CASKET CACHE

A Spencer Funeral Home
Niagara Cozy Mystery

Book 1

Janice J. Richardson
CANADA

Casket Cache
ISBN 978-0-9952395-1-7
eISBN 978-0-9952395-0-0

Cover design by Jennifer Gruhl—
www.facebook/art4ever by Jennifer

Editing & Formatting by MJ Moores, Infinite Pathways

ACKNOWLEDGEMENTS

Christopher Hitchens started the saying with variations thereof that *everyone has one book in them.* That may well be true. Writing a book is almost easy. You write what you know. However, getting the book ready for readers is impossible without the help of others who know much more about books than the author.

Thank you Barb and Pam and Colleen and MJ who proofed, edited, formatted, made suggestions and provided much needed insight. Thank you Twitter friends who provided input on the cover.

Cynthia St. Pierre (*A Purse to Die For*) your encouragement and expert advice spurred me on. It is your generosity of spirit that helps fledgling authors move forward. Merci Cynthia.

1

"We have a coroner's call," Jennifer said to her assistant Peter. "Bundle up, the police say we have a bit of a walk through a field."

"Will do," he said. "See you in a few minutes."

Jennifer disconnected the call, tucked her phone into her pocket and took the stairs two at a time into the apartment above her funeral home. It was almost 11 p.m. and the wind was howling and screaming, scattering and swirling the powdered snow. With the wind chill hovering around -20C she wasted no time putting on her snow pants, parka, and heavy winter boots. She placed her wool scarf on the chair by the door, picked up the thrummed mittens her sister had knit her and pulled on a toque. She was used to the cold but when she was tired it was harder to cope. She reminded herself that she had wanted nothing more than to be her own boss, own the funeral home and stay independent.

"Living the dream," Jennifer muttered as she clumped over to the kitchen counter in her boots, snow pants swishing. Reaching for the cat treats she shook the bag. Grimsby, her black and grey mix appeared like a silent apparition out of nowhere.

"You get to stay warm and comfortable while Peter and I do all the work," she said, scratching behind her pet's ear. "Here's your treat, we should be back in a few hours." She closed the door to the apartment, not bothering to lock it. Downstairs she went straight to the garage, plucked the transfer vehicle keys off the rack and hit the garage door opener.

The icy blast, as the door opened, made her catch her breath. Realizing she had forgotten her scarf, Jennifer considered heading back upstairs to get it, but changed her mind at the thought of climbing the stairs in her snow gear.

As she started the van, she saw Peter's truck pull up through the swirling snow. Climbing out, he reached into his truck bed and pulled out a toboggan, tucked it under his arm, and entered the garage. "We might need this," he said.

"Good thinking."

Peter was the first employee she hired upon acquiring the funeral home two days ago. She'd advertised for a part-time employee and many had responded. Peter stood out; he interviewed well. Peter had a diploma in social media and, in addition to being self-employed, he now worked part-time for Jennifer.

"This is the worst storm I've seen in years," she said, opening the back of the van and watching Peter place the toboggan on the stretcher.

"I haven't seen it like this since I was a kid," replied Peter. "It's not fun driving and it's very cold. Thanks for the gear."

Jennifer had given Peter her uncle's old snowmobile suit and boots just in case the situation warranted it, and this night clearly required it. The climate in the Niagara peninsula was temperate, snowsuits seldom left the closet.

Climbing into the van, Jennifer reached for the GPS and punched in the coordinates for the location the Niagara Regional Police dispatcher had given her as Peter eased out into the blizzard. She knew the general area and the road they were to attend, but having the exact spot mapped would make it easier. She recalled her uncle telling her about some of the calls he'd responded to over the years, remote locations without the benefit of a GPS or cell phone. She was grateful for the technology that made her job easier.

She hadn't counted on the GPS on her phone not working. The device was next to useless with the weather. The blasts and swirls of snow reduced visibility to a few feet and Peter was forced to keep the speed down. She was used to winter, having grown up in northern Ontario. It was just common sense, one didn't go out on nights like this, unless of course, one had no choice.

Six months ago Jennifer had been working at a large funeral home in Toronto. She'd graduated from Funeral Service education at Humber three years before. Working as a junior director in the Greater Toronto Area meant regular shifts with little to no overtime and full benefits. The funeral home had a large staff to share the workload. She'd made new friends and was enjoying her job. The concerts and restaurants and night life were a far cry from the small northern community she'd left behind.

Her uncle was the reason she had become a funeral director. She'd spent several summers as a teen helping him around his funeral home in Niagara. His quiet and gentle demeanor was very different than the home she grew up in. Jennifer had welcomed her summers in Niagara with her uncle and his wife. It was Uncle Bill who encouraged her to find her own way in the world, to make her own choices and not be who her peers and parents expected her to be.

Uncle Bill died suddenly one evening, in his funeral home. Closing up after a visitation, he sat down at his desk and slipped away from a heart attack. Aunt Jean, died of cancer a few months before Uncle Bill and his grief, silent and unspoken, may have been the contributing factor in his death.

Jennifer missed them both terribly, the void the two left in her life was bigger than she thought it could ever be. It made her realize how important her career choice as a funeral director was. Grief, crushing and devastating, was something she had experienced upon the death of her aunt and uncle, and she vowed that as a funeral director she would never forget how hard it was for the families she served.

Uncle Bill and Aunt Jean made Jennifer and her twin sister Anne the beneficiaries of the funeral home and their cottage in the will. Uncle Bill's lawyer contacted the two women, set up a meeting and explained the inheritance. In their grief she had not fully grasped the significance of what the lawyer said. An interim director had been hired by the lawyer to run the funeral home until a decision was made. Her twin, Anne, had taken a different career path. The funeral home wasn't part of her summers, she wanted to be a journalist and upon graduation from university had moved to Ottawa to pursue her dream. She and Anne, although identical in appearance, were polar opposites in personality. Jennifer was social and outgoing; Anne was a loner who loved to research and write. Jennifer made the decision to run the funeral home and share the profits with Anne.

Jennifer thought about texting Anne to see how her day had been but a glance at the dashboard clock changed her mind. Anne liked her privacy and they had an agreement not to disturb each other after 11 p.m. or before 8 a.m. unless it was an emergency. In spite of the poor reception, she texted her friend who was about to start an evening shift at the casino. Gwen was a dealer; a smart, bubbly person who enjoyed her job. She worked the night shift in order to spend time with her husband and family. She and Jennifer usually checked in once or twice a week to see what was new and spent as much time together visiting, shopping, and chattering as their work allowed. She trusted Gwen with her life secrets and Gwen did the same.

Jennifer was surprised when her phone cheeped back a couple of minutes later. Gwen was at work, she said that several people hadn't shown up because of the storm, including the pit boss. The casino was busy, she texted, and they were short staffed. The weather had little effect on the twenty-four hour operation of the resort; people stranded in hotels in the Falls could easily get to the casino. Jennifer texted back: *Don't work 2 hard. Catch U later.* Then slipped her phone back into the inside pocket of her parka.

The falling snow enveloped the road and their vehicle in a white cocoon. Visibility was limited to a few feet, and Peter was concentrating on his driving. The cab was quiet as they both stared at the road ahead. It had been forty-five minutes since they left the funeral home and Jennifer suspected they were getting close to the scene. It was hard to tell where the side of the road was and most of the signs were obscured by the blizzard. The isolation of the storm surrounded them in a peaceful respite.

As was typical in a snowstorm, they were upon the police vehicles almost instantly. The blue and red flashing lights barely broke through the whiteness. Peter maneuvered the van between two police cars and stopped. Jennifer watched to see if someone exited the vehicle ahead but there was no movement. She gathered her mitts, pulled on her toque and jumped at the sudden banging on the driver's side window. Peter lowered the window; the officer peered at them through the fur on his parka, his face barely visible.

"Don't think you'll be able to drag the stretcher through the snow. Check it out." He disappeared as suddenly as he had appeared. Peter flipped his hood up, putting on his gloves as he exited the van. Jennifer slid out her side, wrestling with the door as the wind caught it. She felt like a little kid as she walked around the front of the van where the two men, who were both over six feet, towered over her. She saw the crime scene command post vehicle parked in front of the first squad car.

"How long have you been waiting?" Jennifer

asked. It was her standard greeting to police officers when she attended coroner's calls or house calls. It was not uncommon for police to wait hours at a death call. Waiting for the coroner, the forensics team, the funeral directors, it all took time to facilitate.

"It wasn't snowing when I got here," was the response. Brevity seemed to be this officer's choice of communication style and Jennifer understood perfectly. The man had put in a long shift and just wanted to get out of the snow and cold. He turned and headed into the storm. Heads down, Jennifer and Peter followed. Talk was pointless, the wind snatched the words away. Jennifer followed in the footprints of the two men, struggling with the length of their stride. For every two steps they took, she took three and it was hard to keep up—the snowdrifts a challenge to climb.

About six minutes later they stopped in what appeared to be a small grove of trees. The storm was quieter in the cluster of trees and there was not as much snow. Jennifer noted that a blue tarp had been manipulated into a makeshift tent. Two spotlights provided some light. Several officers stood with their backs to the wind beside the tarp. Flashlights in hand, they watched as the trio approached.

"Detective Sergeant Gillespie," one of them said to Peter.

"Peter. This is my boss, Jennifer," he said turning to her. The Detective Sergeant looked down at Jennifer. The police coats made the men indistinguishable; to her they were all tall, and with their faces buried they all looked the same. But a pair of blue eyes twinkled and a crooked grin greeted her. She responded in kind, surprised at the warmth he exuded.

"Um, we, um, brought a toboggan," she stammered, immediately embarrassed by her lack of *boss behaviour.* She was in charge of the transfer and acting like an apprentice director.

The Detective Sergeant's grin widened. She couldn't tell what colour his hair was, the hood blocked that, but she was acutely aware he was a good looking man.

"A toboggan sounds like a plan," was the response.

Peter stepped in before Jennifer could embarrass herself further. "I'll go get the two-man stretcher and the rest of the equipment," he said.

"Bring an extra sheet," said Jennifer. Turning back to the Detective Sergeant Gillespie she asked "Hiker?"

The Detective Sergeant shook his head no. "Homicide."

Again Jennifer cringed inwardly, the crime scene unit command post should have been a giveaway, not to mention the suit and shoes on the victim. Hiking in a suit and shoes in a field? She needed to stop trying to chat and compose herself. If she couldn't sound professional at least she could try to look professional.

"Hang on Peter," she said, walking over to the tarp. A man lay on his side. He was wearing a suit, no coat. His shoes were shiny and his tie loosened. His cuff links and tie clip looked expensive. Fingertips were black from the ink the forensic team had used, but she quickly surmised this person was a professional: his nails were manicured, his hair trimmed to perfection.

"Bring the kit too please," she said. Peter nodded and he and the officer who walked them in disappeared quickly into the snow.

Jennifer studied the scene carefully. The victim lay on grass and twigs, indicating that the body had been found earlier in the day. There was a single gunshot wound to his forehead. No blood, just a small hole. Except for the obvious cause of death, he could have been sleeping. Every transfer, every individual who required Jennifer's services touched her in some way. A life lived and finished, some too soon, imprinted themselves on her soul.

"We don't have an ID yet," said Detective Sergeant Gillespie, who had moved up behind her. "Recognize him?"

Jennifer turned to the Detective Sergeant and shook her head. "No. We're in the middle of nowhere, who found him?" she asked.

"We got an anonymous tip. Been on the scene all afternoon and evening."

"Long day for you and the team." She knew though, that they would have been well-supplied with coffee and food, an absolute must in the extreme cold. They could take shelter in the Command Post vehicle.

"Are we going to the Falls or St. Catherine's?" she asked, surmising they were more or less equally between the two hospitals.

"Hamilton," he replied. "Case of this nature warrants a forensic autopsy." Without further explanation he continued. "Let me just clarify your information. Jennifer and Peter, right? Last names? Spencer Funeral Home? Do you have a cell number?"

Jennifer provided the information and decided that Peter could drive the van into Hamilton. He would be accompanied by a Detective Constable. She also realized she could be riding in the squad car with one of other two men waiting at the scene, the forensics officer or the Detective Sergeant. It was safe to speculate it would be the officer with the forensics team so she walked over to him.

"I don't believe I caught your name," she said.

"Doug," The fact that Doug didn't look a day over nineteen crossed her mind.

"Are you originally from the Niagara region?"

"Naw, grew up in Cape Breton. Moved here for university and was hired on last year."

"That's a trip I plan on taking at some point," Jennifer responded, forgetting her decision a minute ago to try and stop chatting. "The Cape Breton trail, Nova Scotia, looking forward to seeing the Atlantic Ocean."

The conversation lagged for a minute. "Has your family been to visit yet Doug?"

"Yep, took 'em to the Falls last summer." Another pause. It crossed Jennifer's mind she needed to admit defeat, that none of the men were prone to small talk.

Fortunately, Peter and the other constable materialized out of the blizzard with the equipment and he and Jennifer got to work. Jennifer guided her new employee through what to do at a homicide scene. Donning gloves and removing two paper bags from the kit, she showed him how to bag the hands. They wrapped the body in the sheets and moved the deceased into the body bag. The transfer was a bit awkward under the tent but they worked smoothly together. She removed her gloves and dropped them in the body bag, glancing at Peter who followed suit. She zipped open the stretcher and they placed the body inside. Doug, the forensics officer, stepped in and placed the police seal over the zipper of the body bag. Jennifer then zipped up the stretcher, pulled her mittens from her coat pocket and put them back on.

"I would like you to drive to the hospital in Hamilton," said Jennifer quietly to Peter. "This is your first coroner's call and since it's a homicide, the Detective Constable will stay with the body until it's in the morgue and will tag the pouch once you have arrived. It'll be a long night—are you up for it?"

Peter nodded affirmatively, his eyes briefly betraying his excitement. Jennifer knew he would quickly become a reliable and trustworthy employee. His calm demeanour and interest in learning would serve him well, and give her the occasional night or weekend off from doing transfers in time. He and Jennifer had talked at length about confidentiality and consideration for families; Peter had shown the level of maturity Jennifer expected from her staff.

"The toboggan is a bit shorter than the stretcher but I think if we put the head over the top and go slowly it would save having to carry the stretcher through the snow," said Peter. "If it doesn't work then the kit can go on the toboggan and the officers can help us carry the stretcher."

Doug stepped in to help Peter place the stretcher on the toboggan. The other constable had been watching Detective Sergeant Gillespie working under the makeshift tent. He was checking for evidence that might have been under the body and ensuring that nothing was missed. Jennifer and Peter stood quietly and respectfully while the task was completed.

"Ok, let's get going," said Detective Sergeant Gillespie.

Peter pulled the toboggan in the direction of the van. Jennifer walked beside the toboggan, ready to jump in should the stretcher start to slide off. Doug walked on the other side. Detective Sergeant Gillespie was giving final instructions to the constable at the tarp.

In spite of the terrain and snowdrifts, it was an easy trip to the roadside. Jennifer opened the van doors and bent down to pick up the side of the stretcher.

"I got it ma'am," said Doug and he and Peter placed the stretcher in the van. Jennifer picked up the toboggan and placed it on its side away from the stretcher.

"Thank you. Appreciate the help," said Jennifer "I've been thinking, with you two officers and Peter going to Hamilton I think I'll check to see if I can get a ride back to the funeral home. Peter will be able to take care of things from here."

"I'll check," said Doug as he reached for his

radio. He walked away from the vehicle so Jennifer couldn't hear the conversation. Doug quickly returned. "No problem, just wait here."

Peter had finished brushing the snow off the windows of the van and left a couple of minutes later, followed by Doug in the forensics officer's car. Jennifer stood looking at the remaining two police vehicles covered in snow, and wondered if she should start clearing the snow away. She trudged over to the command post and, using her mitts and sleeve, started pushing the snow off.

She had almost completed the squad car when she heard voices. Detective Sergeant Gillespie and the other constable were exiting the field.

"You're still here Ms. Spencer?" asked the Detective Sergeant. Jennifer was a little taken aback, she knew Doug had cleared her ride home with one of the officers.

"I sent Peter to Hamilton with the two officers. I understand this isn't normal procedure but I'd appreciate a lift back to the funeral home. Doug, your forensics officer, cleared it with you?"

"Huh," responded Detective Sergeant Gillespie. He smiled with that endearing crooked smile. "Doug did." He turned to the remaining officer. "Goodnight Constable."

The young man looked at his vehicle and turned to Jennifer. "That was very kind of you to clear the snow ma'am. Thank you."

"No problem."

Detective Sergeant Gillespie unlocked his car and opened the passenger door. Jennifer, feeling a little self-conscious, thanked him. He popped the trunk, placed his gear in and, pulling out a brush, finished clearing the snow off the car. Jennifer sat very still, lost in thought as she waited. She found herself feeling a little awkward when Detective Sergeant Gillespie took the driver's seat. It wasn't her first homicide, she knew the routine, but sitting next to this blue-eyed police officer with the crooked grin made her feel vulnerable. She chided herself for her silliness and chalked it up to fatigue.

It didn't take long for the vehicle to warm up and Jennifer pulled off her toque and mitts. The snowstorm was letting up; visibility was better than it had been earlier. But Detective Sergeant Gillespie had yet to speak and Jennifer wondered if she should initiate a conversation—then decided against it. As a child she'd had a habit of filling space and void with chatter and had learned, as a funeral director, to let silence do its job.

As they got closer to the main highway Detective Sergeant Gillespie broke the quiet.

"Are you settling into your new home?" he asked.

"Slowly. It was such a shock when Uncle Bill

died. I think he was grieving Aunt Jean more than we realized."

"I got to know your uncle a bit over the years. He was a good man, well-respected in the community."

Jennifer nodded, but before she could reply a car shot out into the intersection ahead. She instinctively braced for impact as Detective Sergeant Gillespie scrambled to avoid a collision. The police car skidded but held the road. The car that cut them off disappeared into the night.

Gillespie cursed. Jennifer's heart pounded at the near miss and she exhaled slowly. He reached for the radio and reported a vehicle speeding down Townline Road, make and model unknown.

"Taurus," said Jennifer. He related the information to the dispatcher and turned back to her.

"Are you OK?" he asked, the concern in his voice obvious. "Are you hurt?"

"I'm fine."

"You're sure?"

Jennifer nodded.

"I apologize for my language. What an idiot; he could have killed us. Can't believe you got the model of the car."

Jennifer laughed weakly. "Comes from driving miles a day through Toronto. Kinda got used to getting cut off and all the near misses. Where are the police when you need them?"

His burst of laughter broke the tension. Jennifer joined in and in a couple of minutes the stress of the moment left. They could hear the radio chatter and it wasn't long before the driver who cut them off was pulled over.

When they arrived at the funeral home a few minutes later, Jennifer let herself out of the squad car and thanked the Detective Sergeant for the lift.

"Good night," said Jennifer.

"Good night."

She wondered what his first name was as she opened the door. No point, she said to herself, you're way too busy to think about anything other than work. Entering the funeral home, she pulled her phone from her pocket. A quick check showed it was after two in the morning. She made a mental note to debrief Peter later in the day. She could still recall every detail of her first homicide years ago and wanted to be sure Peter wasn't traumatized. She didn't want her new employee emotionally damaged by what he'd seen and done. She'd discuss the scene, the transfer, and the victim as she so often did with her colleagues in circumstances like this sudden death.

The snow had built up around the garage. She picked up the shovel and went to work on the sidewalk. The quiet of the night and the soft light from the snow was peaceful. Jennifer worked slowly, enjoying the physical labour and peace.

Twenty minutes later she put the shovel away, laid out the supplies for the next call, left a note with the call details on the front desk, and headed up to bed. She'd call Peter in later in the day. Grimsby met her at the door. After Jennifer had a quick shower, she and her cat crawled into bed.

2

Jennifer woke with a start and for a brief moment didn't know where she was. As the fog in her head cleared, she remembered the coroner's call the night before. She rolled over and looked at her phone. It was a few minutes after 9 a.m.

"Grimsby, we slept in." Grimsby yawned widely, every tooth showing. He looked at his mistress slit-eyed, put his head down and ignored her.

Sitting on the side of the bed, Jennifer reached for the landline that connected her to the answering service for the funeral home and the internal funeral home system. She kept the ringer off at night, the answering service called her on her cell phone if she was needed by a family or the police after hours. She hit the button for the front office.

A cheerful voice greeted her. "Good morning Jennifer. Coffee's on. I see you had a coroner's call last night."

"Thanks Elaine, we did. I'll be down in a few minutes."

Elaine had worked for her Uncle Bill for over

fifteen years and had watched Jennifer grow up. For as long as Jennifer could remember, Elaine had been a constant at the funeral home. She ran the front office, comforted families, many of whom she knew, and she kept the funeral home spotless. She had stood beside Jennifer and Anne at her Aunt Jean's funeral and again at Uncle Bill's. Jennifer loved her like family.

Donning her black jacket, white blouse, and grey striped skirt, Jennifer worked her hair into a bun. She slipped her ever present cell phone in her pocket, checked Grimsby's water dish and food, and picked up her parka and snow pants she had hung on a hook by the door the night before. Taking them downstairs she hung them in the garage, noting with satisfaction that Peter restocked the van. She walked to the front of the funeral home.

Elaine rose as Jennifer approached and the two of them headed to the lounge for coffee. Jennifer had installed a new coffee system, one that could brew several pots of coffee in quick succession. Elaine put a tea bag in a cup and poured hot water from the spigot, Jennifer helped herself to the fresh pot of coffee. The bar fridge held milk and creamers. The two moved to a grouping of club chairs and sat down.

"You look tired hon," said Elaine kindly.

"I was back by two. Peter was awesome; he's a quick study. He took the body to Hamilton."

"Do you know who it was?" asked Elaine. "Anyone local?"

"Don't know. No ID. Should be in the news soon enough."

The phone rang and Elaine rose to answer it, this time heading to Jennifer's private office off the lounge which was discretely hidden behind a plain soundproof door. Jennifer placed a call to Peter from her cell. His wife, Angel, answered the phone and agreed to send Peter in once he was up and mobile.

Jennifer sat back and looked around the familiar setting. In the few days since she had legally assumed responsibility for the funeral home, she still had not become used to the fact that it was hers. There was a lot to learn and Jennifer had tried not to let it overwhelm her. Elaine had been invaluable, helping with the bookkeeping program, reviewing the inventory and list of suppliers, outlining the vehicle leases and service contracts.

Elaine emerged from the office, phone in hand. "It's a Detective Sergeant Gillespie for you," she said handing Jennifer the phone.

"Good morning," Jennifer said. The next few words popped out of her mouth before she realized how stupid it sounded. "Did you sleep well?" She cringed, embarrassed by her familiarity with the officer.

"Grabbed a few hours," he said smoothly, as if

Jennifer's faux pas was perfectly normal. "Thought you might like to know who the driver was of that car that cut us off."

"For sure," she responded, wondering again if she had a professional bone left in her body. Every time she opened her mouth around the handsome Detective Sergeant she sounded like a kid.

"Travis Holden."

Jennifer was at a loss to respond. Travis Holden was the director who covered the funeral home for the three months following Uncle Bill's death. She had worked with him the day before she took over, in order to catch up on what funerals he had done and what needed her immediate attention. Uncle Bill's lawyer, Mr. Duncan, had hired him via a service that supplied ad-interim funeral directors. To her knowledge, there had been no complaints about him from the families he served.

"Oh," she said, her mind racing. "Was he charged?"

"Ticketed for running a stop sign," Detective Sergeant Gillespie said. "He had a previous for careless a few years back."

"Thanks for letting me know."

"No problem." He disconnected the call.

"What was that all about?" asked Elaine.

"Travis. He nearly hit the police car the Detective Sergeant and I were riding in last night.

Ran a stop sign. They pulled him over a short while later."

"That's interesting," mused Elaine. "He didn't strike me as the type to do anything reckless, but then again ..." Her voice trailed off.

"Then again?" asked Jennifer. "Did you suspect him of something? Did you know him?"

"No, No," said Elaine, quick to reassure Jennifer. "He did a good job here. The families seemed to like him, he was respectful. I didn't work very much, he would send me home if there were no calls, he preferred to run the place by himself." She paused.

"But?"

"Oh, it's nothing. Just an old lady's suspicious nature."

"Come on Elaine, it's intuition, not suspicion. And you aren't old. What gives?"

"It's just that he seemed to have an edge to him, like an undercurrent of restlessness the last few weeks he was here." Elaine shrugged. "Just a feeling, that's all."

They chatted for a few minutes about their lives and when Jennifer finished her coffee, she rose. "I'd better get busy, have to shovel again," she said. "Thanks for making the coffee."

The funeral home was on a corner; the parking lot could be accessed from two streets. The chapel door was at the side of the building, the garage at the back, and the front door faced the main street with a covered portico drive-through to drop people off. A plowing service took care of the large lot, leaving the sidewalks to be done by the funeral home staff.

She put on her coat and boots and headed outside. The sunlight was reflecting and dancing off the snow in sparkling lights. She took a deep breath and surveyed the landscape. Winter was her favourite time of year. But, in a few short weeks it would be over.

The snow was light and fluffy, and as she shoveled she reflected on her conversations with the Detective Sergeant and Elaine. She made a decision to check on Travis' Board Standing when she got back inside. The Board that regulated Funeral Services kept records of directors who had faced disciplinary action for misconduct or more serious charges. Perhaps, she thought, Travis had been driving recklessly because there was no traffic. She too had been guilty of speeding once in a while, she just hadn't been caught.

The mailman was walking down the side of the road just as she finished the front walkway. The sidewalk plow had yet to go by, a not uncommon problem in the southern part of the province. Up north the sidewalks were plowed and the streets often cleared before dawn. There, with the winter season being longer, the municipalities had the equipment.

"Good morning," said the mailman as he handed her a small bundle. "It's cold eh?"

"Indeed," she replied. "Be careful walking." She headed around the building to the garage entrance, stamped the snow off her feet and put the shovel inside. Elaine entered the garage just as she was removing her coat.

"There you are," she said. "I was just coming to get you. You have a call."

Jennifer took the slip of paper from Elaine. "She is a hospital chaplain," said Elaine.

"Thanks." Jennifer headed to her little office off the lounge. The phone was answered before the second ring.

"Chaplain's Office, Regina Salinas speaking."

"Rev. Salinas, this is Jennifer at Spencer Funeral Home."

"Thank you for getting back to me so quickly," said the chaplain. "Please call me Regina. I have been working with a family and I'd like to discuss their situation with you."

"Of course," replied Jennifer.

"This is a young couple who were expecting their first child. Sadly, the baby will be stillborn. The mother is to be induced later today. Our team has discussed options with both of them, and the father, Matt, would like to meet with a funeral director.

Would you be available to come to the hospital in an hour?"

"I can meet you at your office, Regina. Perhaps you and I could have a few minutes to get acquainted and discuss the parent's wishes."

"I will be here. Thank you."

Jennifer buzzed Elaine in the front office to let her know she would be leaving in about an hour, and turned to her computer. She logged onto the Board of Funeral Service site and checked to see if Travis had any disciplinary action against him. Nothing.

She sat back in her chair and pondered for a few minutes. Picking up the phone she called Mr. Duncan's office and asked his secretary if she knew what agency the lawyer had used to hire Travis. The secretary promised to get back her later in the day.

Jennifer's cell phone chimed. It was Gwen.

"Hi Gwen, aren't you supposed to be sleeping?"

"Ya. Dropped the kids at school, picked up some groceries and did a laundry. Just wondered if you knew anything about a possible murder. Rumours are our pit boss was killed."

"Really?" replied Jennifer. "What did you hear?"

"Apparently, he was found dead. Someone said he was in his car, another one heard he was somewhere near a vineyard."

"Was that the same boss you couldn't stand, the

one you tangled with over that rude customer he wouldn't deal with?"

"Yep. He was not on my list of favourite co-workers, a real jerk. Of course, I have rude customers all the time. Comes with the job. He didn't always stand up to them and support his staff. Most of the dealers disliked him."

"I can't place him," said Jennifer, her mind racing. She'd occasionally visit Gwen at the tables when her friend was working. Once a month Jennifer and the girls would drive down from Toronto, go to the casino, have dinner, see a show, and play a bit. She had really looked forward to those outings.

"Big guy, buzzed hair, always in expensive suits," continued her friend.

Jennifer knew immediately the coroner's call the night before was him. She couldn't let Gwen know, it would be a violation of confidentiality.

"Anything in the news?" she asked calmly.

"Nothing yet," her friend said. "Not much information."

"Let's catch up later," said Jennifer. "I have a meeting shortly. Call me when you get up, if you hear anything. Sweet dreams."

"K—bye." Gwen disconnected.

Jennifer put the call out of her mind and prepared to meet with the young couple who had the pending stillbirth. No death was easy, miscarriage, stillbirth, infants, child, teen, adult, they all affected the survivors lives permanently.

Driving to the hospital she reflected again on how her life had taken such a major turn. Her job in Toronto was fulfilling and she had been happy there. She had no responsibility except to the families she served. Now she had a business to run, a bottom line to respect and maintain, staff who depended on her for a job. With so many details involved in running a business, Jennifer knew she had a tough road ahead. Her personality suited her career choice, she was compassionate and she genuinely cared about the families she served. She also recognized that although she was a social, outgoing individual, she didn't trust easily. Uncle Bill knew many people in town and could comfortably carry on conversations about their kids and jobs and their lives. Jennifer found that lately she preferred a book and cherished her quiet time. She also had little business training; she needed to take some courses and was quickly discovering the needed to find a balance between her private life and new business life.

Pulling into the hospital parking lot she smiled wryly to herself. Plenty of time to sort out the changes, she thought. If Scarlett O'Hara could think about it tomorrow, so could she. She loved all things related to the movie *Gone with The Wind.*

As she entered the chaplain's office an attractive lady with black hair looked up from the counter. "Jennifer Spencer to see Rev. Salinas," Jennifer said.

The lady rose and extended her hand. "I'm Regina, Jennifer. Come, we can talk in my office."

Regina led the way to a small, cluttered office and closed the door. "Let me tell you about Matt and Amber."

Jennifer listened intently as Regina passed on the information about the unfortunate young couple. They lived in a northern community. This was their first child. Amber started to experience problems shortly into her fifth month of pregnancy. An ultrasound revealed the stillbirth and Amber had been immediately transferred to a tertiary care facility by air, arriving the evening before. Regina had met with them several times and remained on call, sleeping at the hospital should they ask for her.

"Matt would like to speak with you about what their options are. He's leaning towards cremation."

"What about Amber?" asked Jennifer. "What are her wishes?"

"That's hard to determine. Matt wants to protect her and I think she hasn't been able to process her feelings yet about what comes next."

"I would like to meet with them both. That is, I would prefer to see them together, maybe after I speak with Matt. I feel that Amber needs to be part

31

of the decision and they should both be in agreement."

Regina nodded affirmatively. "We are on the same page there. Let's go. I'll introduce you." Together the two women headed up to the maternity floor.

Regina stopped at the nursing station to let the staff know that she and Jennifer would be with Amber and Matt to discuss the baby's arrangements. Amber's room was at the end of the hall. Tapping gently, Regina pushed the door open. Immediately a young man jumped to his feet. Jennifer noticed he looked exhausted and strained.

"Amber, Matt, this is Ms. Spencer. She's the funeral director I told you about." Jennifer extended her hand; Matt shook it abstractly.

"Let's go outside," said Matt. Jennifer glanced at the young woman in the bed. She was pale and quiet. She showed little response to her husband's request.

Turning to Matt, Jennifer said, "Of course. You can fill me in then we can discuss it between the three of us in a few minutes."

"I'll sit with Amber while you two talk," said Regina as she sat in the chair Matt had just vacated.

"The sunroom is empty; shall we talk there?" asked Jennifer as they left the room. Matt seemed to be a bundle of nervous energy. He had trouble looking straight at Jennifer and he paced as he talked. Jennifer sat quietly while he explained that he didn't want his wife upset any more than she was, and he needed to know if they could just have the baby cremated and go home.

When he paused, Jennifer asked gently, "Does your baby have a name?" Matt startled and looked at her with a mix of surprise and anger. "We were going to name him Aaron. But it doesn't matter now." His shoulders dropped a bit and Jennifer felt his despair.

"Matt, I'm here to respect and honour the decision you and Amber make about Aaron. The next day or so will be very challenging for the two of you. I understand Amber will be induced shortly?"

Matt nodded.

"I'd like you to know that there will be no charge for my services. The crematorium will also waive their fees. It may be a day or two before the hospital releases Aaron because of the autopsy. I will take care of the details and bring Aaron's cremated remains back to the funeral home. If you wish, I will send them to you by courier."

"This makes no sense. She was doing just fine. I don't want cremated remains, I wanted my son. Now I just want this behind me."

Jennifer let the silence hover for a bit. Decisions made quickly in Matt and Amber's situation could result in unresolved grief and she was not going to rush him into a discussion about the baby's cremated remains.

The silence lingered, the air heavy as Matt struggled with his emotions. Jennifer continued to sit in silent support.

"Amber doesn't need the stress right now," reiterated Matt. "I don't want the cremated remains."

"I agree," said Jennifer. "You and Amber do not have make that decision right now. I will keep the cremated remains at the funeral home for the next year and then contact you if I haven't heard from you and Amber. But let's include Amber in this discussion. I want her to have a brief chat with me, since I am the person who will be looking after Aaron once the hospital releases him."

Jennifer half expected Matt to protest but as she rose, he followed her into the room. Clearly Regina had prepared the couple for challenges they might face over the next few days and months. Matt wanted to keep his wife from any more stress and grief, and Jennifer appreciated that the young man cared so much about her.

"Amber, honey, this is the undertaker," said Matt. Jennifer had not taken her eyes of the pretty young woman in the bed. Stepping forward, she touched Amber's arm.

"I'm Jennifer. Matt told me about the decision

the two of you made for Aaron."

At the mention of the baby's name, Amber teared. "We just want this over with so we can go home," she said.

"Understood," said Jennifer. She paused until Amber looked at her. "Do you and Matt want to go ahead with cremation?"

Amber nodded.

"Then, as I explained to Matt, I will ensure your wishes are carried out. There is no charge for any of the services, and I will keep Aaron's cremated remains at the funeral home until you are ready for them to be sent to you."

"We don't want them," said Amber dully.

Jennifer caught Regina's eyes. The chaplain remained silent; Jennifer knew she supported holding the cremated remains until the couple was ready.

Jennifer pulled her business card from her pocket. It was the first time she had used it and she knew this call would stay with her for the rest of her life. The shiny black letters that said *Spencer Funeral Home* with her name below hit her hard.

She placed the card on the nightstand. "Do you have any questions Amber?"

Amber shook her head no. "Matt?" She turned to the young husband.

"No," he responded.

"I can be reached at any time if you need me or have any questions. I am so sorry. This is such a difficult time for the two of you." She looked over at Regina, her eyes signalling the end of the conversation.

Regina rose. "I'll be back in a few minutes," she said to Amber and Jennifer.

Jennifer touched Matt's arm gently as she rose to leave the room. Her eye contact was brief and she hoped he saw the compassion she was trying to pass on.

In the hall, Jennifer handed Regina her business card. "I have the information you gave me, I will draw up the contract and leave it with you later today or first thing tomorrow morning. I expect Amber and Matt will be leaving late tomorrow if the induction goes well?"

Regina nodded. "I'll ensure it is signed. Perhaps I could drop it off?"

Jennifer cocked her head slightly. That wasn't quite what she had expected and she rather liked the idea of meeting with Regina at the funeral home.

"That would be appreciated. Thank you for all your help."

Regina gave Jennifer a tiny smile and turned back to the hospital room. Jennifer left the hospital, sober and saddened by the young parents' ordeal.

3

Elaine rose as Jennifer entered the funeral home. "How did it go?" she asked.

"The chaplain was very kind and she paved the way for me to discuss the death with the parents," responded Jennifer. "I'll draw up the contract as soon as I have lunch. Anything new here?"

"Several messages. Why don't you eat and let me get the contract ready and print it? I have the messages here." She handed over several pink slips.

"Thanks Elaine." She was used to doing her own contracts but knew that Elaine was more than capable. Having her staff do more than asked was taking some adjustments. "Here are the details—I'll be upstairs."

Closing the door to her apartment, Jennifer exhaled deeply. Grimsby rubbed up against her, chirping softly.

"Hey bud." Grimsby followed her to the kitchen, and as Jennifer prepared her sandwich and tea she refreshed Grimsby's water dish and offered her pet a treat. One of the staff at the rescue centre had given her advice about training cats and Jennifer had taken it to heart. She randomly presented her cat with treats and did not maintain a routine other than making sure her cat had food and clean water. That ensured that Grimsby didn't waken her or insist on being fed before dawn. Sleep was a precious commodity in a twenty-four hour a day operation.

Sitting at the table, Jennifer checked the messages. One was from a family who called to let the funeral home know a death was imminent. The funeral had been prearranged by Uncle Bill several years before, and Jennifer knew Elaine would have put the file on her desk. She'd review it when she got downstairs. Another was from a supplier confirming delivery time for a casket, and she realized Elaine had reviewed the prearranged file and ensured the casket was restocked quickly.

The final message was from the funeral home she had worked at in Toronto. It was from Marcia, one of her colleagues and a good friend. She had Marcia as a contact on her cell phone; she was puzzled as to why she hadn't texted or called. She dialed the funeral home number from memory and settled back in her chair.

The receptionist recognized Jennifer's voice immediately. "Jennifer! How are you? How are things at the funeral home? Have you been busy? Are you settling in? Do you like the Niagara region?

Have you made any friends yet?"

Jennifer laughed at the barrage of questions and she as the receptionist caught up on each other's lives for the next few minutes. An incoming call at the busy Toronto funeral home ended the conversation. "Let me get Marcia for you; don't be a stranger," said the receptionist as she put her on hold.

"Marcia speaking."

"Hey! What's up?" said Jennifer, happy to hear her friend's voice.

"Jen! I have a surprise. Got room for an old friend?"

"You're coming down? Really? When?"

"Later this evening if that's OK with you. I have a transfer to a funeral home in the Falls, the boss thought it might be a good idea to send me to spy on you." Marcia laughed happily. "I don't have to bring back the van back until late tomorrow."

"That's great! I can't wait. But—"

"But what?"

"I have a pending death, actually, two of them; so I'll have to stay close to home."

"Not a problem my friend. I'm at your disposal."

"Nice play on words," Jennifer said dryly. "I can't wait to see you."

"Me too. Gotta scoot home, throw my stuff in a bag, and get back here to pick up my transfer. I wish we could complete the triumvirate, maybe next time. See you sometime tonight."

"Ok, drive safely," said Jennifer as she hung up. She felt her mood lighten significantly at the thought of an overnight visit with Marcia. While the other part of the threesome, Phil, wasn't coming this time, she knew the three of them would get together at some point soon. Phil had graduated with Marcia and had mentored Jennifer her first year at the funeral home. The three of them had worked through some busy days together and always looked out for one another. They called themselves the triumvirate, even though they knew they took the true meaning of the word out of context.

"Grimsby, you are in for a treat. Marcia's coming." Grimsby's tail swished slightly and Jennifer wondered if it was Marcia's name or her voice he was responding to. It was Marcia who encouraged Jennifer to visit the shelter, and it was Marcia who suggested she and Grimsby might be a match. Jennifer had been reluctant to get a cat, or any pet for that matter, but her friend had been right. Grimsby had settled in quickly and helped stabilize Jennifer during the past few weeks.

A buzzer sounded, alerting Jennifer that there was a delivery at the garage door. She put her dishes in the sink and headed down. Opening the door, she met the casket truck driver, who introduced himself and handed her the delivery slip. Jennifer hit the button for the overhead door and was just about to introduce herself when Elaine entered the garage. The driver greeted Elaine by name.

"Have you met Jennifer?" Elaine asked.

"Was just about to," the driver responded, extending his hand. "You are the new owner? Welcome to the region."

"Nice to meet you. And thank you for the prompt delivery." She didn't mention that this was her first casket delivery, that she had never dealt with such details before other than watching Uncle Bill help unload a few times. The funeral home in Toronto took care of those details, she and the other directors just took the casket they needed from the storage room and someone else, probably the manager, took care of such purchases.

The church truck was off to the side, Elaine pulled it over and between the three of them the casket was offloaded in a minute. There were several other caskets on the truck, the driver was partway through his route.

Elaine offered the driver a coffee.

"Thanks Elaine—next time. It's my daughter's birthday and I want to get home early."

As the driver left, Jennifer made a mental note to call the locksmith later in the week. The locksmith had changed all the locks except the one on the garage door, that one was on back order and should have arrived by now. As an added measure of security, the locksmith had put an inside latch on that door. The funeral home did not have a security system. She'd lived in Toronto long enough to become cautious. In a small community a break in wasn't as much of a concern, but she didn't want to risk it and she hoped within a year to have a monitored security system installed. Changing the lock would do for now. It dawned on her that Elaine could make the call. Turning to her, Jennifer asked if she'd check with the locksmith.

"I'll get right on it," she said. "The contract from your call this morning is completed and on your desk."

"Thanks. I'll take it over to the hospital right now. Be back in fifteen minutes."

Jennifer donned her coat, plucked the car keys from the rack and headed out, this time with no boots, hat or mitts. It was still cold but with the snow cleared, getting around was much easier and the hospital lot would be the same.

Regina was not in the office when she arrived. Jennifer introduced herself to one of the other chaplains. He was a pleasant older gentleman with a British accent, who introduced himself as Clive, and reassured her he'd see that Regina received the envelope.

Back at the funeral home Jennifer headed to her office to review the prearrangement file. Elaine had left a note saying that the lock for the garage was still on back order but the locksmith hoped to have it within a week. And the lawyer's office had left a message with the name of the Funeral Director's Service that Travis worked for. Jennifer could hear the vacuum running, Elaine enjoyed keeping the funeral home spotless, a never ending task all the staff shared in.

Once she had reviewed the file, Jennifer took care of a few other minor administrative details and then checked the time. She and Elaine moved the casket for the prearranged funeral into the prep room and put the new replacement on the bier in the selection room. Marcia would be arriving soon and Jennifer felt a rush of excitement at seeing her friend. She decided to take her out to dinner rather than prepare a meal. She might even be able to have a glass of wine. It wasn't something she was able to do very often now, the chance that she would have to meet with a family on short notice usually precluded a drink. The last thing she needed was to have someone notice alcohol on her breath.

Elaine interrupted her train of thought as she entered the lounge. "Anything we need to get done before tomorrow?"

"Nope. We're ready for whatever happens. My friend Marcia is coming down for the night and I think I'll take her out to dinner this evening. See you tomorrow."

"Goodnight, have fun," responded Elaine as she went to get her coat. A few minutes later Jennifer heard the door chime as Elaine left.

Jennifer readied the funeral home for night mode, leaving a few lights on. She had started leaving lights on at night, because to her a dark funeral home just looked creepy from the outside, and in. Should she have to come down in the night to do a transfer, the light made it feel safer and more welcoming.

She had barely finished making the bed in the second bedroom when her text notification went off. It was Marcia, letting her know she was at a gas station in town and would be there shortly. Jennifer quickly changed into her jeans and a sweater and headed downstairs. From the window she watched for her friend in the growing darkness. The front street was quiet, no traffic, and only one car parked on the side of the road. It looked like there was an occupant in the driver's seat but it was hard to tell. There was no mistaking the shape of the car though, and Jennifer felt a tiny tug of fear. It was a Taurus. She shook her head. I can't react every time I see a Taurus, she told herself. There are too many out there and it's not likely that one belongs to Travis. He's probably off on another assignment.

Headlights from a slow moving vehicle came into view and Jennifer could see at once it was the Toronto Funeral Home van she and Marcia had spent many hours in. She opened the front door of the funeral home, waved happily and pointed to the side street. Marcia was already making the turn as Jennifer closed and locked the front door then half ran to the open the garage door. The two friends hugged, both talking and laughing at once.

Once they got inside, Jennifer asked her friend if she had trouble finding the funeral home.

"I googled it on street view, it looks just like the picture," said Marcia. "Quaint. Love it."

"Come on up." They climbed the stairs to her apartment. Marcia greeted a waiting Grimsby, who allowed her to pick him up and hug him. Jennifer could hear him purring as he settled into her friend's arms. She picked up Marcia's overnight bag and headed to the small bedroom. "This is your room. We share a bathroom. As you can see, this is the living room and kitchen. My room is at the back."

"I recognize your furniture. It fits nicely here."

"Thanks. One of these days I might change the paint colour in the kitchen to something a little softer. I like the blue but it's not me. You hungry?"

"Getting there. I stopped at Timmies just before

I left to pick up the van and haven't eaten yet." Marcia was referring to Tim Horton's, a popular Canadian chain of coffee shops. When doing a transfer, leaving the vehicle for coffee was not an acceptable practice. If it was a long drive, usually two funeral home employees would go, leaving one to stay with the vehicle and the body. Even with an unmarked van, going through the drive thru was against company policy. One of the support staff had done just that and had been reported to the funeral home by an off-duty director who recognized the vehicle, resulting in the loss of his job. It was all about respect for the deceased and the family.

"I have just the place for dinner. It's not far, I need to stay close to home. The food is great. When we get back, I'll give you the grand tour."

"Oh good. Right behind you," said Marcia as she put Grimsby down.

Over dinner the two friends discussed their work, their friends, and their plans for the future. Jennifer was able to share with Marcia the details of the coroner's call. They laughed over her fumbles with the handsome Detective Sergeant. Marcia brought her up to speed with Phil's antics. They were just about to indulge in a gooey caramel chocolate dessert when Jennifer's phone rang.

"That's the answering service. Let's take the

dessert with us."

"I'll do the transfer with you."

"Haven't you worked enough today?" asked Jennifer as they waited for the bill.

"Haven't you? I'm coming."

"Then you drive us back to the funeral home. I'll call the family."

"Spoken like a true boss," said her friend as they left the restaurant.

Jennifer spoke with the family member who had called and confirmed that visitation could start the following afternoon.

Dropping their purses and dessert in the garage, Jennifer handed Marcia a black overcoat. It dwarfed her friend.

"Hmmm, I think we are ready," said Jennifer. Marcia made a face at her. "Well, at least you can't tell we are in jeans."

As the two of them started to climb into the van, Jennifer stopped. "I'd better put the keys for the car back on the rack," she said. Marcia laughed. "I think that might be a good idea." While there were spare keys in the safe, putting things like keys back in the proper place immediately could make a difference. It was easy to leave a set of keys in a pocket of a coat or jacket and spend hours looking for them a day or so later. Marcia had done just that when she was an apprentice, it held up the funeral she was working on and the funeral home constantly reminded staff to pay attention to details. Both women knew how the little things could make a difference.

As Jennifer walked over to the key rack, she thought she heard a thump behind the wall. She paused for a second to listen. Must be hearing things, she thought. She hit the overhead door button and they headed to the nursing home.

The home was close, and twenty minutes later they pulled back into Jennifer's garage and hung up their coats.

"I'll put our lady in the prep room," said Jennifer. "Why don't you head up and relax?"

"Sure," said Marcia picking up their purses and the dessert. "Tea?"

"Sounds good, thanks." As she offloaded the stretcher and entered the back hall to the prep room, Jennifer noticed a slip of paper on the floor. Puzzled, she bent over to pick it up. A glimmer caught her eye. The tile floor had a spot of water, as if someone had tracked snow through. She froze. Maybe the thump she'd heard earlier was an intruder. The slip of paper had not been on the floor when she and Elaine had moved the casket into the prep room.

"Marcia!" she yelled, her voice betraying her fear.

Within seconds her friend was at her side. "What? What's wrong?"

"Look," said Jennifer in a shaky voice. She pointed to the floor.

Marcia looked puzzled. Jennifer continued. "The floor's wet, like someone walked through with their boots on. And look. This was on the floor. She showed Marcia the slip of paper. "I thought I heard a thump before we left. There was someone here." She paused, trying to slow down her breathing and her pounding heart. "Maybe they're still here."

"Let's get this lady into the prep room and call the police," said Marcia.

Jennifer nodded, still trembling with fear as she dialed 911. The dispatcher assured them the police would be there shortly.

Jennifer let her friend guide her through the next few minutes. Once they had moved the deceased into the prep room and made sure the door was locked, Marcia broke the silence. "The footprints seem to end at the selection room. Don't touch anything."

"Marcia, I want to get a picture of this piece of paper. Can you do it? I'm too shaky."

Moving to the garage Marcia put the paper on the hood of the van and snapped a photo. It contained some letters and a number. Jennifer stared at it, her mind racing.

"Jennifer. Jennifer!" Marcia called, breaking through her fog. "We need to unlock the door for the police."

Marcia barely finished her sentence when they heard pounding on the garage door. Marcia led the way, Jennifer followed on wobbly legs. She felt nauseous and distant, as if the events unfolding before her were just a dream.

"Who is it?" Marcia shouted.

"Police."

"Wait Marcia, let me check to be sure." Jennifer went to the chapel window. There was a squad car parked near the garage; Jennifer headed back.

"It's OK," she said.

"That was a fast response time," muttered Marcia as she unlatched and opened the door. One officer stood there and Jennifer could see a second squad car pulling in.

"Ladies, I understand you reported a possible break-in?"

Marcia held the door open for the second officer. The cold air and response to her fear made Jennifer's shaking worse. She nodded, afraid to trust her voice. The police presence hammered home the reality of what had taken place. She felt violated. Her new home and business wasn't the safe place she thought it to be.

The second officer, a female, spoke up, "Let's sit down and you can tell us what happened."

Jennifer nodded again, led the way to the lounge and turned on the lights. Marcia quietly went over to the counter to make tea. The officers declined tea and coffee, so Marcia made some for Jennifer and herself.

"Your name?" said the first officer.

"Jennifer Spencer. This is my funeral home."

"You took over from Bill Spencer? Your uncle?"

"Yes." The officer turned to ask Marcia's her name and if she was an employee. Jennifer barely heard the discussion, she was still numb.

Marcia gave the officers the details of what had happened after they returned from the nursing home. Jennifer sat quietly, sitting down with tea had helped ground her. She added the part about the thump she thought she heard as they were getting ready for the transfer.

"What room do you think it was?" asked one of the officers.

"Part of the selection room is right behind that wall," said Jennifer. "It doesn't make sense."

The officer looked at his partner, and then at Marcia. "Do you think you could show us what you found?"

"Of course," said Jennifer, strength returning to her voice. She led the way to the door to the prep room hallway.

"Thanks. You can wait with your friend. We will probably have more questions shortly."

"Wait," said Jennifer. "There's a client in the

prep room. Do you have to go in there? That door was still locked when we got back from the nursing home."

The officer hesitated. "We might. I'll let you know."

Back in the lounge, Marcia rose from her seat and gave Jennifer a strong hug. "It's OK."

"I'm so glad you're here," said Jennifer, tears stinging her eyes. "Thank you."

They sat in silence for a few minutes. Jennifer was the first to speak.

"Grimsby! Oh my gosh. What if he went upstairs?" Jennifer didn't even notice she had said *he*. She sprang to her feet; Marcia following suit.

As they went toward the apartment the female officer stopped them.

"I'm sorry, we need you to wait in the lounge," she said

"My cat. I need to check on him."

The officer shook her head. "Not yet, we have work to do."

Marcia frowned. "We have work to do as well, there's a funeral tomorrow and we need access to the prep room." The officer and Marcia stared at each other.

"Please, take a seat. I will check with my partner," said the officer.

As the officer headed towards the back hall,

Marcia scooted into the garage and grabbed the cake box. With a giggle she pushed Jennifer back to the lounge.

"It's a stand off. This could take a while. Let's eat."

Jennifer laughed in spite of herself. Marcia had a way of making even the bad times manageable.

They were finishing their cake when the officer returned.

"It is going to be a while," she said. "There will be some more officers joining us shortly."

"Who?" responded Jennifer.

"The identification team," said the policewoman. "We have asked our supervisor if it is possible to give you access to the prep room. We also have to check your apartment before we can let you enter. Did you check the rest of the funeral home to see if anything had been moved or is missing?"

"Not yet," responded Jennifer. Marcia and Jennifer looked at each other. "I'll help you with the prep," said Marcia. "Grimsby will be fine; he knows where to hide."

"Grimsby?" said the officer.

"The cat," responded Marcia, her matter of fact tone making it seem as if everyone should know that Grimsby was a cat. The officer's mouth twitched with the hint of a smile.

"Are your prints on file Marcia?" asked the

officer.

"With the Toronto police. I didn't touch anything in the funeral home other than in the garage and apartment."

"Like my friend said, if we can have access to the prep room that would be appreciated," said Jennifer. "Tomorrow will be a busy day and we need to get our work done."

The officer nodded. "I will be back in a couple of minutes so we can do a walk through the rest of the building."

As the officer left, an idea pushed itself through Jennifer's brain fog. "Let's check the safe."

4

Unlocking the office door, she flicked on the light and looked around. Nothing appeared to be disturbed. Marcia stood quietly behind her while she opened the safe door. The contents were as she left them. Jennifer sank into her desk chair, Marcia sat across from her.

"What was that person doing here?" Jennifer mused. Marcia just shook her head.

"Maybe we should take advantage of this time to review tomorrow's funeral," said Marcia.

"Good point." Jennifer realized her friend was trying to keep her grounded. For the next few minutes the two funeral directors organized their day. Peter and Marcia would pick up the funeral coach and the family car they leased from Williams Funeral Home, the other funeral home in town. Jennifer had a meeting in the morning with Regina Salinas, the chaplain from the hospital; she had left a message for her earlier that afternoon to notify her of the afternoon funeral. The minister who was doing the funeral would be picked up by Peter. Marcia and

Jennifer rechecked the file to ensure they had covered all the details.

Once they were both comfortable with the plan, Marcia sat back and looked at her friend. "I wonder what those numbers and letters on that slip of paper mean?" Jennifer shook her head. "Maybe it means nothing, or maybe it has something to do with why the person broke in," Marcia speculated.

"I wonder how much longer do we have to wait to get into the prep room?" Jennifer chuckled weakly. "We have to stop 'wondering' and get on with it," she said. The words were barely out of her mouth when she saw two police officers enter the lounge.

The female constable spoke first, "We need you to tell us if anything in the room where the caskets has been disturbed. First, will you walk us through the rest of the funeral home and apartment? We can finish at the prep room, once that is cleared we will let you proceed with your work."

"I can wait here," said Marcia. Jennifer looked at her friend and raised an eyebrow. "Then again," Marcia said as she got to her feet. "I might as well come along."

The two officers and the two directors did a thorough walk through of the main floor. Nothing appeared to have been tampered with or missing. The apartment was just as they had left it. Grimsby was snoozing on the back of the couch. He ignored the group of humans walking through his space.

Back downstairs, they entered the selection room where the identification team was checking the caskets for fingerprints. Jennifer frowned. Black dust was all over the handles. It could be easily removed from the metal and wood caskets but not so easily from the cloth ones. The bedding in the caskets had been ruffled through. Something clicked.

"Marcia—the piece of paper—it's a casket model," she exclaimed.

"I would never have guessed. The manager does the ordering where I work."

"It's the casket number for the one in the prep room. The new one, the replacement came today, I put it in the selection room. What would this person want with a casket? How did they get in? Who is it?"

Jennifer walked over to the newest addition to the selection room and looked at it closely. She asked the officer if anyone had checked inside. The officer confirmed that they had taken a cursory glance inside each casket.

"Do you suppose they were interested in that casket in the prep room?" asked Marcia.

Jennifer swiveled and walked to the prep room, pulling out her keys. With the officers behind her as she entered, she was thankful that she and Marcia had followed protocol by covering the deceased on the prep table with a sheet. Since she was usually the only one in the funeral home it would be easy to let things behind the scenes slide once in a while. She made a silent vow to herself to continue not to disrespect the deceased or neglect procedures, even if she was tired or rushed.

Jennifer stopped herself just as she was about to touch the lid of the casket. She turned to the officers and asked if the identification team needed to dust the handles or lid. The officer nodded.

"I'll be right back," she said.

The identification officer didn't take long dusting the casket. He lifted the prints, which Jennifer suspected were hers, and asked her to inspect inside. Marcia walked over to the glove box and pulled a pair of surgical gloves, handing them to her friend. Jennifer donned them and raised the casket lid.

Jennifer handed Marcia the pillow. As Marcia inspected and squeezed it, Jennifer lifted the material and started sifting through the cotton and kapok. She brushed an object and withdrew her hand quickly. Feeling a little foolish she reached back into the bedding and pulled out an open envelope. She started at it mindlessly for a few seconds before she realized it was full of thousand dollar bills. Lots of pink and brown thousand dollar bills. No one spoke as Jennifer handed it to the officer. He immediately left the room with it.

The other officer watched as Jennifer finished her inspection of the casket. She even looked at the bottom, not sure if she would find another envelope taped underneath.

"OK ladies," said the officer. You can get to work now. She smiled at them as she closed the door.

Marcia and Jennifer exhaled simultaneously.

"Wow," said Marcia quietly. "Who knew your new life would be so exciting."

"That was a lot of money. This is getting strange." Pulling her best Scarlett O'Hara impression, she said, "I can't think about that now, I'll think about it tomorrow." Her impression of Vivian Leigh always made her friends laugh.

The two girls donned lab coats and gloves and immediately got to work. About a half hour later, a few minutes into the start of the injection of embalming fluid, a tap came at the door. Jennifer stripped off her gloves and opened it a crack.

"Miss Spencer, we need to speak with you," said the officer.

"I got this," said Marcia. "You go."

Just as Jennifer was often curious about police procedures, she suspected the officers were just as curious about what she did. Nonetheless, she didn't open the door farther. "I'll be right out," she said. Removing her lab coat and washing her hands, she slipped out, grateful that Marcia was there to help.

Jennifer led the way to the lounge. The other officers we getting ready to leave but the female officer followed her colleague and Jennifer into the lounge.

As they were seated, Jennifer's stomach clenched and felt the conversation wasn't just about their findings. Their body language made her uncomfortable. She felt the need to be proactive.

"Do you have any idea who might have broken in?" she asked the male officer.

He looked at her steadily and the silence seemed endless.

"Do you have any idea how the money got into the casket?" he responded, parroting her need to stay on top of the discussion.

"No." She decided quickly if the conversation wasn't going to be give and take, then it was an interrogation and she wasn't going to volunteer information, other than the truth in as few words as possible.

"Are you sure?"

"Absolutely." Jennifer held his gaze.

The silence thickened as the officer studied her demeanor. Jennifer's heart beat faster than it should, she hoped it wasn't showing.

"Is the money yours?" said the officer, trying another tack.

"No."

The officer continued to ask questions about Jennifer's whereabouts during the day. She told him she had been to the hospital and the nursing home and out to dinner, volunteering only the times and locations.

Frustrated with his questions, Jennifer decided it was her turn.

"What can you tell me about the break in?" she asked.

"Someone, possibly male, entered your casket room looking for that envelope. Did you know it was in the casket?"

Nice try thought Jennifer to herself.

"No." Jennifer wondered why he called it a casket room when she made it clear it was a selection room.

"Well, Ms. Spencer, we will let you get back to work. I will be in touch when we have further questions. Here's my card."

He and the female officer rose as Jennifer took his business card.

"Thank you," she responded and she walked them to the door.

As the door closed behind them Jennifer latched it then leaned up against the garage wall. She still felt a little detached and shaky. She stood quietly, breathing slowly and deeply with her eyes closed, trying to ground herself. A few minutes later she opened her eyes and headed to the prep room.

Marcia looked up as she entered. "Almost done, we can casket her in the morning. What did the officer tell you?"

"He had nothing to tell me other than they thought it was a male looking for the money. They were more interested in trying to get me to confess to putting the money there."

Marcia raised an eyebrow and responded with, "Well. Did you?"

Jennifer burst out laughing, Marcia joined in.

"I have a bad feeling it could be Travis. Who else would write down a casket number, and know where to go when they came in?"

"If I had that much money I be spending it, not hoarding it. Shoes," mused Marcia. "Lots and lots of shoes." The two laughed again, Marcia loved shoes.

Twenty minutes later, having completed their work and not come any closer to solving the mystery, the two friends headed upstairs. Grimsby greeted them, happy to let Marcia pick him up and pet him.

"Guess he'll be sleeping with you tonight," said Jennifer as they headed to bed about twenty minutes later, Grimsby on Marcia's heels. "Goodnight."

"Goodnight."

In spite of the stress and excitement of the day, Jennifer was asleep quickly.

Waking before the alarm the next morning, she quietly slipped out of bed and headed to the kitchen to start the coffee.

By the time Marcia wandered out of the spare room, all sleepy and rumpled, Jennifer was dressed, showered, and ready for the day. She handed Marcia her coffee and went to put on her makeup before starting breakfast. Jennifer had made a point of trying to eat a decent breakfast over the past week, recognizing that lunch and/or supper might not happen if the events of the day got away from her.

"I'm going down to set up the visitation room. See you in a bit."

"K—" mumbled her still sluggish friend.

It was a beautiful sunny day. The snow was nearly gone and a quick glance at her phone showed her the temperature was going to be a comfortable 7C. It was 8 a.m.

Jennifer set up the flower stands, made sure the room was in order, and unlocked the prep room to check on the deceased. She and Marcia could do the casketing and transfer to the bier when she came down, or she could wait until Peter arrived. The flowers would be arriving mid-morning.

Standing back to survey the room, Jennifer felt a rush of pride. Last night's incident had not affected her sleep; she knew there was nothing more she could do to solve the problem. She was more interested in the tasks at hand, her visit with the chaplain and taking care of the family and the funeral.

She headed to the lounge to put the coffee on for the staff. As she unlocked the front door she heard Marcia humming to herself as she walked down the hallway.

She turned to her friend. "You know, I've been thinking about our funeral suits. Would having a plain navy or grey suit for days when there isn't a funeral be a better idea than wearing stripes all the time?"

"I like wearing a funeral suit all the time," said Marcia. "But I am inclined to agree with you. When you are running the funeral home and doing all the tasks, it's hard on clothing. It's easier at the funeral home in Toronto, we don't do a lot of the grunt work, like wash cars and shovel snow and garden. Navy would be a good colour for you."

"Tradition is important to me, and people expect high standards from funeral directors. Appearance matters. When I hire another funeral director I'll give it serious consideration. In the meantime, I might look for a navy suit to see how I like the idea. Anyway, I'm going to pop over to the grocery store and pick up some juice and soft drinks. The family will be here at twelve-thirty, they might like something other than tea or coffee. I'll be back in about twenty minutes. Elaine should be here anytime soon."

"OK. I'll hold the fort."

As Jennifer headed to the garage she wondered if Marcia would consider coming to the Niagara region to work. Jennifer's uncle had run the funeral home with support staff and she was recognizing that Aunt Jean had been the reason for him being able to do so. Having another director on staff would ease the strain of the 24 hour/7 days a week treadmill she was on. Aunt Jean made sure the daily minutiae were taken care of, leaving Uncle Bill to do what he was licensed to. Aunt Jean cooked, cleaned, shopped, banked, did the laundry, helped around the funeral home, assisted with visitations and for the most part, supervised the support staff.

Jennifer parked the Lincoln at the side of the grocery store and headed straight to the orange juice. Rounding a corner, she almost didn't see the man pushing the grocery cart coming the other way. It was a near miss.

"Sorry," said Jennifer, glancing up. A familiar face with a crooked grin met her gaze.

"Ms. Spencer."

Jennifer could feel the redness creeping into her cheeks. "Detective Sergeant Gillespie," she responded.

"Have you recovered from the excitement at

your place last night?"

"Not sure. Haven't had time to process it." Wow, she thought, news travels fast. Of course he would know about it; it wasn't every day one found money in a casket.

"So you're busy?" The Detective Sergeant was chatty. Jennifer realized she didn't know his first name, and for a fleeting second wished they were on a first name basis.

"Yes. Have a couple of calls right now." She paused, then moved back to the break in. Maybe he had some information for her. "The officers last night didn't have any information."

"Neither did you from what I hear," said Sgt. Gillespie.

Jennifer looked at him sharply. "What do you mean by that?" she responded, trying to keep the anger out of her voice. "Am I a suspect?"

"Should you be?" was the laconic response. Jennifer felt her anger rising. She took a deep breath. What was it about this man that brought out the worst in her?

He threw back his head and laughed. Once again she felt silly and small beside him. It gave her something else to get defensive about.

"Ms. Spencer," he began.

"Jennifer," she interrupted. "Call me Jennifer."

"Jennifer," he said slowly. "You live alone?"

Why did he ask that question, she thought and then, why did I give him my first name? He was probably married.

She nodded.

"Be careful," said the Detective Sergeant. "Call us if anything happens or if you see anything."

Anxious to make her escape, she started down the aisle. "OK—thanks!" she said as she picked up the orange juice and headed to the cash register.

It wasn't until she was a block away that she remembered the soft drinks. The Detective Sergeant had a strange affect on her ability to focus. I seem to fall apart around him, she thought. He didn't give me his first name. I have to stop letting this man get to me. Should I be worried about the break-in? He didn't answer my question about me being a suspect. Am I? For that matter, how did he even know the details? What business is it of the homicide department?

Pulling into a convenience store she bought some ginger ale, chiding herself for letting her awkwardness with the Detective Sergeant get the better of her. It had been a few years since she had been in a serious relationship. Being a funeral director made having a significant other difficult: Long hours, having to be professional and compassionate in the face of tragedy, burn-out and fatigue, the physical and emotional challenges of the profession, helping people carry their grief, and the unpredictability of death in a twenty-four hour day spared little time for family. It took a special person, like Aunt Jean, to be able to support and understand why a funeral director chose to enter into such a demanding profession.

Next time I see him, if there is a next time, I'll be as distant as possible, and say as little as possible she said to herself. My career comes first. No time for Detective Sergeants with crooked grins. In spite of her resolution, her heart jumped a bit at the thought of his laugh when she questioned him about whether or not she was a suspect. Come to think of it, she thought wryly, he was composed and distant. He didn't even answer me. "Move on Jennifer, move on," she said out loud as she pulled into the funeral home parking lot.

Once inside, she and Marcia had time to visit quietly for a bit. Jennifer wanted to broach the subject of asking Marcia if she'd consider working with her, but thought it best to wait until she'd discussed it with her twin.

Promptly at 10 a.m. Rev. Salinas arrived and Elaine ushered her into the upstairs office. Elaine and Marcia busied themselves around the funeral home.

"Thank you for stopping by Regina," said Jennifer as she entered the office and closed the door.

"How are you doing?"

Regina's warm smile made Jennifer realize how Regina's clients would be comfortable with the chaplain. "I'm doing well, thank you. I see you are busy today."

"Indeed," Jennifer replied, returning the chaplains smile. "Did Amber and Matt return home?

Regina nodded. "They will be leaving later this afternoon. It's such a sad event for a young couple to go through."

They spent the next few minutes talking about the situation. Regina then steered the conversation to Jennifer's funeral home and asked if she could have a quick tour.

"I'd be delighted." Jennifer rose. "You can meet the staff and my friend from Toronto who's visiting. She was a big help last night when we had the break-in."

"Break in?" Were you here? Are you OK?"

"We were at dinner when the person broke in, and we are fine. Last evening, I was quite shaken but a good night's sleep does give one a new perspective."

She introduced Jennifer to Elaine and Marcia, took her on a tour, omitting the prep room. As they walked by the suite that was in use, Regina paused at the door and looked in.

"Beautiful setup," she said. "This is a

comfortable, warm room for families and their guests.

"Thank you," said Jennifer, touched the by the chaplain's kind words. As they entered the lounge, Peter put his cup down and stood up.

"Morning boss," he said with a grin. "Came a little early to see if you needed me but I guess you guys got it all done."

Jennifer laughed. "I have Marcia to thank for that. I see you and Marcia have met. This is Chaplain Salinas; Regina, this is Peter."

The two shook hands. "Tea or coffee Rev. Salinas?" asked Peter. Jennifer was delighted to see Peter's respect and proactive approach.

"Tea please, just milk." Regina took a seat.

The next half hour was filled with laughter and chatter. Eventually Peter and Marcia excused themselves to pick up the funeral cars and Elaine left for the front office.

"You have a great staff and a lovely funeral home," said Regina. "I appreciate you taking the time to show me around."

"My pleasure. Please, stop by anytime, and feel free to bring your colleagues."

"I will. Most of them knew your uncle, I never had the privilege."

At the door Regina gave Jennifer a quick hug. "I hope they find the intruder. You stay safe."

"I'll be careful. Thank you for dropping off the paperwork."

Jennifer let Elaine know where she would be and headed up to her apartment to start making a batch of sandwiches for lunch for the staff. Coming down the stairs with the tray she heard voices in the lounge: Peter and Marcia were deep in conversation, with Elaine listening in. Lunch was quick and after tidying up Jennifer excused herself and went upstairs to call her twin, hoping she'd answer her phone. Anne did pick up, with an abrupt, "Yes?" No hello or hi, her *yes* was the typical answer when she had a phone call and didn't wish to be disturbed, which was most of the time.

"It's me. Did I wake you?"

"Nope. What up?"

Jennifer smiled. Short and to the point, just the facts ma'am responses.

"How's work?"

"Good."

Giving up was easier than dragging information or conversation out of her sister, so Jennifer came right to the point.

"I have an important question for you."

The silence indicated that her sister was listening and expected Jennifer to continue. She knew it was easy to mistake Anne's abruptness for indifference. Nothing could be further from the truth,

71

Anne had sharp instincts and excellent listening skills. That's what made her a good reporter.

"The funeral home is a handful for one person," said Jennifer. "I knew it would be 24/7 and I am fine with that. However, I do think I need another director. Marcia would be a good candidate."

"What about an apprentice?" asked Anne.

"Not sure I'm ready to take on a student and if I do, the student can't make arrangements unless I'm on site. It would be at least six months before they could do so even with supervision."

"Well, do what you want. It's your call."

"Alright, thanks. Let's talk when you have time and see if we can't get together in the next month or so."

"Sure. I suppose I could come down for a visit. I just don't want to watch you work all the time I'm there. I want to have some fun."

"Fair enough. I'll let you know what Marcia decides to do. It'd be perfect if she could move here. Talk to you soon."

No goodbye from Anne, she just hung up. End of the conversation. Jennifer was social, Anne was intellectual. Jennifer muddled through decisions, Anne was decisive. Anne was a night person, Jennifer welcomed the day early and with energy. A perfect twenty-four hour us, thought Jennifer. I miss her. She sat quietly for a few minutes thinking about her decision. Grimsby jumped up beside her and Jennifer abstractly rubbed his ears.

A tap at the door interrupted her thoughts. "It's open." Marcia entered.

"Just going to put my stuff in the van, I'll be heading out right after the funeral," she said.

"OK. But before you do, can we talk for a minute?"

"Of course," said Marcia, puzzled by the seriousness in Jennifer's voice. She took a seat at the end of the couch.

Jennifer took a deep breath and decided to jump right in. "Would you consider moving to Niagara and working with me? I can't pay as much as we made in Toronto, but the cost of living is better and I'd really like to have you on board."

"Wow," said Marcia. "I wasn't expecting that."

"I know. I didn't mean to spring it on you. It's just that, well, I can't think of anyone else I'd rather have here. You're perfect for the position. Take your time with the decision, and let me know when you're ready."

"I am ready," said Marcia seriously.

Jennifer took a deep breath.

"On one hand, I have a great job in Toronto, regular hours, good pay, great people to work with. If I move here, I have to find a place to live, work longer hours at times and have great people to work with. I was considering a position on the west coast." Marcia made a balancing movement with her hands. Up, down, up, down. Jennifer exhaled, the air heavy with anticipation.

"When do I start?"

5

The rest of the day went quickly. The funeral was flawless; Jennifer was proud of the way her staff worked as a team. Peter took direction well for his first funeral, ensuring the cars in the procession had their lights on, assisting the family to the car, then standing quietly beside the family car, looking quite handsome in his new funeral suit which the tailor had finished the day before. Marcia instructed the pallbearers, loaded the casket and stood at the funeral coach, hands folded until Jennifer opened the door of the lead car for the minister, moved to the driver's side and nodded at them to proceed. The pallbearers' car was driven by an employee of Williams Funeral Home on the other side of town where they leased the cars. Three of the pallbearers drove their own cars to the cemetery.

Jennifer's heart was thumping as she started the procession. Every time, without fail, she had anticipatory anxiety when leading a procession. It was a type of performance anxiety and it was always unpleasant. She had occasional nightmares about processions in which she would be driving around and around cemeteries trying to find the grave, or driving for miles, unable to find the cemetery. Those nightmares would jolt her awake, heart pounding.

She covered her anxiety as best she could, not allowing it to overwhelm her or get the best of her, but struggling with the intense discomfort took a lot of emotional energy out of her. Even if she knew every inch of the cemetery, she would secretly review the route over and over on the hand drawn map she kept in her pocket for every funeral she led. Her counsellor in Toronto had suggested that short of taking a tranquilizer, that might be the best course of action.

Jennifer did not want to take meds, it dulled her senses and she needed to be alert to every potential misstep during a funeral. The anxiety wasn't going to kill her. It was just unpleasant. The worst of her fear was thinking about getting started, once she became involved in the process her anxiety eased. She didn't feel truly safe until she pulled up to the graveside.

She used the time driving the procession to get acquainted with the pastor sitting beside her. A few leading questions were all it took for him to start chattering about his church, the family, himself. She did her best to appear to listen intently and to give the impression that leading a procession was as simple as walking down the street. Nothing could be further from the truth, she thought wryly to herself. If I never lead another procession it would be too soon, but since no job is perfect, it has to be done. She frequently glanced in the mirrors to check the activity behind her. Marcia's experience exceeded hers and she was perfect on coach, staying slightly right so Jennifer would have a better view from the side mirror as to what was going on behind her. Only Marcia and Phil knew how she struggled with her fear and they had supported her without minimizing or diminishing the reality of the panic attacks.

As always, once the procession pulled up to the grave, Jennifer's anxiety started to alleviate. Peter stood quietly beside the family car and Marcia beside the coach while Jennifer placed the flowers. The pallbearers took their place at the coach. Peter opened the door to the family car, assisting them out. Jennifer stood with the family and the minister as Marcia led the pallbearers to the grave.

Jennifer loved this part of a funeral, if one could *love* such a difficult time. It was a time of tears and pain and the beginning of closure. She recalled Uncle Bill's funeral, how she had sobbed at the graveside, her grief freely releasing itself.

Once Marcia had placed the pallbearers she returned to the coach and pulled away. She would meet Jennifer back at the funeral home after she took the coach back, using her cell phone's GPS for guidance. Jennifer stood beside the minister, the committal sander in her hand. When the brief committal service was over and the minister stated "earth to earth, ashes to ashes" she leaned over and made the sign of a cross on the casket. Some families were not religious and if they did not wish to have a traditional service the committal sand might be used, she just didn't make a cross, it was more like a circle. The solemnity of the graveside service always moved Jennifer deeply. She then pulled a couple of roses from the casket spray and handed them to the family.

If there was going to be a mishap at a funeral, the graveside seemed to be the place. Pallbearers slipped, flowers blew away, mourner's fainted, or worse. She was still the boss and in charge, and it required her undivided attention.

As the mourner's lingered by the graveside, she observed the driver from Williams Funeral Home go back to his vehicle and sit inside, cell phone in hand. While he wasn't out of line staying by the vehicle, the use of the phone was not appropriate. She approached Peter who was standing attentively nearby.

"Do you know the other driver's name? Dimitri, the manager at Williams Funeral Home told me, I forgot it though."

"George, with a J, which would make it Jorge," he said lightly as he spelled it out for her. "He made sure Marcia and I knew it was Jorge, with a J and he spelled it again."

Jennifer smiled wryly at Peter's sarcastic humour. "Well, Jorge with a J is out of line."

"Saw that. He should be standing near the car, not sitting in it, and his cell phone should be in airplane mode or on vibrate or sleep mode or any mode but on."

"If we have him again, and we undoubtedly will, I'll make sure I let him know for the next time. It's not my place to train another funeral home's staff, but on *our* funerals, I expect better."

She turned back to the graveside and watched as a few mourners walked back to their vehicles. The post funeral reception was to be held at the church; Jennifer would drop the minister off.

The family stood quietly beside the grave, holding hands. A minute later, their final goodbye complete, they turned to the minister. Peter stepped in and walked them back to the family car, Jennifer and the minister beside them. Once the family was tucked inside she and the minister returned to the lead car.

The chatter between the two on the way back was lighter and more mundane. She liked this minister. He was pleasant and not preachy, like some could be. At the funeral home, Elaine bustled around, putting the last of the flower stands away.

"Coffee's on," she said brightly. "How did it go?"

"Great. I was really pleased with Peter. And there were no mishaps, no one fell into the grave."

Elaine laughed. Her years of service meant she had a plethora of some of Uncle Bill's funeral blooper stories.

She helped Elaine finish the few remaining little tasks and the two went to the lounge to wait for Peter and Marcia. Jennifer checked her texts. Gwen wanted to pop by later before work. She answered in the affirmative.

When Peter and Marcia returned, Jennifer took the opportunity to praise him for his work. Marcia concurred and Peter blushed from the compliment. They talked about the other driver's behaviour briefly, Marcia wasn't impressed either. Jennifer and Marcia both believed that after a funeral the staff needed time to decompress. The grief of the family, the attention to detail for visitation and funeral made for a stressful time and she allowed the time to review and chat about the day.

Marcia made the first move. "Gotta run. Boss will be calling wondering when his van is coming back. Bye all—hope to see you soon."

There were cheerful goodbyes from Elaine and

Peter as Jennifer followed Marcia out of the room. At the door Marcia turned to her friend.

"I'll put in my notice. Don't be surprised though if the corporate office has an eye on your funeral home. They're always looking to expand and it would be an important acquisition. I have the feeling our old manager has already started the process."

"He was a good boss, at least with me," said Jennifer.

"Me too. I almost feel like a traitor: working for a corporate funeral home had it's perks. But working here will satisfy my need for autonomy."

The two friends hugged and agreed to chat later that evening. As Marcia pulled away, Elaine answered a call. "It's a gentleman named Phil," she said.

Jennifer took the phone.

"Phil!"

"Hey kiddo, how's it going?" said the third member of the triumvirate affectionately.

"Awesome. It was great to see Marcia. When do I get to see you?"

"Soon I suspect," said Phil. They chatted happily for a few minutes about their lives.

"The real reason I called is to see if Marcia has left yet. We got slammed and need her back tonight."

"She left a few minutes ago. Barring a traffic jam, she should be back in a couple of hours."

"Thank you Ms. Spencer," teased Phil. "I shall inform the powers that be."

"Love you, buddy. Now get to work."

"Yes ma'am. Talk to you soon."

Elaine had approached with another message just as Jennifer ended her call with Phil.

"The hospital called. The baby has been released."

Peter, who was standing nearby, raised an eyebrow.

"The baby is going to the crematorium," she explained.

"May I come?" asked Peter.

"You sure?" asked Jennifer.

"I'm sure. I want to learn and help. I'm sure it's not going to be easy, but when is it easy picking up someone's family?"

Jennifer looked at him for a few seconds before answering, "Alright. We will take the lead car, not the van in this situation. I'll show you where the baby box is that we use for transport."

A silent Peter watched as Jennifer went to the prep room to pick up the baby box. She pulled a receiving blanket from a drawer and explained to Peter that it wasn't really necessary but it was how she had been trained and it just seemed right to her. Peter nodded.

"I will casket him when we get back and take

him to the crematorium in the morning."

She placed the little wooden box her Uncle had used for many years on the back seat of the car. As they drove, Jennifer told Peter to ask any questions he needed answers to, and told him it was important that he find his level of involvement, not hers. Again he just nodded.

At the hospital they picked up the paperwork at the admitting department then drove around back of the hospital to the morgue. Peter continued his silence until they entered the morgue.

"May I?" he asked.

Jennifer looked at him. "Alright." She handed him the gloves she had put in her pocket at the funeral home.

"Why gloves? He's so tiny and new."

"He is. But you always use universal precautions. No exceptions."

Peter put on the gloves, laid out the baby blanket on the morgue stretcher and picked up the tiny bundle. He paused, then gently drew Aaron to his chest. Jennifer, understanding his need to face the little one's death, did not interfere. For a brief second in time Peter cradled Aaron, then gently placed him on the receiving blanket and wrapped him up. Just as gently, he placed him in the baby box, picked it up and walked out of the morgue, Jennifer following. A single tear clung to his cheek; Jennifer remembered her first baby death. She had responded the same way. She had the impression from observing Peter that social media might not be his final career choice. She had seen Uncle Bill break down once or twice and she respected them both for their sensitivity. Peter would make a good funeral director.

At the funeral home Peter watched as Jennifer casketed the baby, turned out the light and shut the prep room door.

"Goodnight," was all he said as he headed to his truck to go home.

"Goodnight Peter." As the garage door closed behind him, Jennifer latched it in place. Elaine had locked up and gone for the night, so Jennifer headed up to her apartment.

Grimsby greeted his mistress like a long lost friend.

"What's gotten into you bud? Miss me? Or are you just waiting for dinner?"

She fed her cat, made herself a salad and a pork chop and sat down to eat. "I feel like I've run a marathon," she said to Grimsby. "The last few days have been so busy." Jennifer knew that she'd remember the past few days fondly. She was delighted that Marcia was coming soon, and relieved that it had been so easy. Being the only director made it challenging and she marvelled that Uncle

Bill had managed with just an apprentice director.

Someday, she thought. Someday I'll bring in an apprentice. Marcia and I will make sure they learn everything they can so they have the opportunity to go anywhere in the country. If I can be half as good as Uncle Bill, I'll be happy.

As she washed her few dishes, her cell phone chimed. It was Gwen, she was stopping at Tim Horton's and wondered if Jennifer wanted a Chai latte. Jennifer texted back with *duh* and laughed out loud. Chai lattes and Gwen were a given, and she went downstairs to watch for her friend, anxious to hear what was happening with the pit boss' murder.

She heard the funeral home phone ring and took a deep breath. If it was another call she might have to cut Gwen's visit short. The answering service would call if it was important. Gwen pulled in within minutes and Jennifer opened the garage door.

Gwen swept into the space like a breath of fresh air. She had a presence wherever she went. Jennifer often asked her how they could be friends, they were so different. Gwen would laugh with that infectious giggle of hers and respond in kind. Polar opposites they were and the respect was mutual.

"Can't wait to tell you what's going on with the PB's murder," said Gwen breathlessly.

"Murder?" Jennifer raised an eyebrow.

"Murder and intrigue," responded Gwen

dramatically as they climbed the stairs.

Fed and content, Grimsby ignored the two chattering females and brushed past them to his favourite spot on the back of the couch. Over their lattes, Gwen told her how most of the dealers and supervisors on the night shift had been interviewed by the police, some more than once. One of the other dealers had been interviewed three times and it was rumoured that he was a suspect.

"What kind of questions did they ask you?"

"Oh, you know, the usual stuff." Gwen waved her hand dismissively and dramatically.

Jennifer laughed. "No, I don't know."

"What kind of relationship we had; how long had I known him; did I know anything about his personal life; did he have any enemies; did I socialize with him outside the casino, that stuff." Gwen stopped to take a breath. "As if. Socialize with him? Did he have any enemies? More like, did he have any friends." She snorted with derision.

"I'm aware you didn't like him, but why?"

"The man had risen to the height of his incompetence. No one liked him. More than once when a customer was being rude or inappropriate and I notified the supervisor, who then passed it to him, he'd shrug it off. Had one guy who was so drunk he was practically lying down on the table. It was four in the morning, really quiet and he just ignored him. If that happened on day shift that tipsy customer would be out of there in a flash."

"I don't know how you do it." She'd said that to Gwen many times.

"I don't know how *you* do it," said Gwen, having said that about Jennifer's choice of career many times as well. "Rumours are he was into something, drugs most likely," continued Gwen.

"No proof?"

"Not yet. The dealer that's under suspicion hung out with him."

"Do you have a new pit boss yet?"

"They brought a guy in from day shift. He's a lot stricter, plays by the book. He probably won't stay; he hates the night shift."

Jennifer's cell phone rang. She looked at her friend with an *uh oh* kind of expression. Gwen jumped up and announced she was heading to the bathroom.

"Ms. Spencer, you had a call from a gentleman about pricing. I have his information, he asked that you call back at 10 p.m."

After writing down the information, Jennifer thanked the service and put her phone down. Gwen joined her again and they inevitably got back to talking about work.

"Anything fun happen at work recently?" Jennifer asked.

"Not really, other than Richard the King."

"Do tell." Jennifer settled back to listen. She loved it when Gwen regaled her with stories about her job as a dealer.

"There was this guy at my table, introduced himself as Richard, talked about himself, how wonderful he was, how much money he made, what kind of truck he drove. I just ignored him and kept dealing. He held up a $5 chip and said to me, "Just say *Richard is the King* and this chip is yours."

"What?" squealed Jennifer. "Seriously? Oh my gosh—what did you do?"

"I leaned over the table and whispered in his ear. My sub tapped me off and I went on my break." Gwen paused, the air poignant with suspense. She was particularly good at telling a story thought Jennifer. Wish I had that gift.

"Oh come on—what did you say to him?"

Her friend's smile grew. "All I said was—you can keep your chip Richard, with an emphasis on the *Richard.*"

Jennifer laughed until the tears came.

"On a lighter note," said Gwen. "How's your job going?"

"Two calls in four days, a coroner's call, a few inquiries. Marcia came down on an overnight visit on a transfer and we had a break-in."

"A break-in? Anything taken?"

"Nothing."

She told Gwen that she had found an envelope with money in a casket and that the police had it. She also told her not to repeat the story to anyone, knowing Gwen would keep the confidence. She didn't tell her it was the pit boss who she and Peter picked up on the coroner's call. The break-in was one thing, discussing funeral home business where a family could be affected was another.

They spent the next hour laughing and talking about Gwen's kids. Finally, Gwen jumped to her feet, ready to start her workday. Jennifer, on the other hand, was ready to curl up with a book before bed.

"See ya," said Gwen.

"Lattes are on me next time," responded Jennifer as she watched Gwen start her car and drive off. The air was chilly and Jennifer, rather than linger and enjoy the night's silence, locked the door, bolted it and headed into her office. It was a few minutes before ten. Her desk was tidy and organized, her work caught up. She looked at the name and number the answering service had given her and checked it against Uncle Bill's records. It was a manual process and Jennifer was pleased that Elaine was working on digitalizing the records. The name did not come up.

Promptly at ten, Jennifer dialed the number. It was answered on the first right.

"Wisener," was the crisp response.

"Mr. Wisener, this is Jennifer Spencer at Spencer Funeral Home. How can I help you?"

"Pricing. I would like to determine how your prices compare to your competition."

He's just shopping, thought Jennifer to herself. Why couldn't he do this during business hours?

"Of course," she responded politely. "What specifically were you interested in? A traditional funeral, burial? cremation?"

"Cremation with one visitation," replied Mr. Wisener. He wasn't making it easy with his short requests. At least I have something to work with, thought Jennifer.

Starting with the transfer from the place of death, she rhymed down the price list. She outlined the range of cremation caskets and their prices and the cost of the visitation. She added that the family could bring in their own visitation book or that one would be provided. She explained that they could project digital pictures and where they could purchase flowers if desired. She then gave Mr. Wisener the cost of the transfer to the crematorium, explained the plastic cremation container that held the cremated remains, giving him the price range for urns if he should want an urn. Not once did he interrupt and she had the impression that Mr. Wisener was like Anne, an attentive and astute listener.

"Any questions Mr. Wisener?" she asked.

"Do you not think you are charging too much for a casket?" he asked.

Jennifer was a little taken aback by his comment. "With a range of cardboard to wood, I think it is fair to say that any family's needs would be met. However, it is possible to purchase a casket on your own and have it delivered to the funeral home. Alternatively, the occasional family will make their own casket. I can provide the specs for the crematorium if that decision is made.

Mr. Wisener was not to be deterred. "Your transfer costs, why so much?"

Jennifer was starting to get annoyed with this man. She knew her costs were in line with the other funeral homes in the area and less than her counterparts in Toronto, a city where distance affected the costs.

"It's calculated on mileage to the crematorium which is a thirty-minute drive, times two, of course, because we pick up the cremated remains and bring them here."

Jennifer hoped that would be the end of the conversation. She was tired and suspected Mr. Wisener would probably not be using her services.

For another ten minutes he drilled her about every detail, and pulling it together, she graciously answered each question. Mr. Wisener had not once mentioned a pending death or a prearrangement, he seemed only interested in her pricing and she wondered if he was from her competition in the region.

The conversation ended with, "That will be all," from Mr. Wisener.

Jennifer responded, "If I can be of further service, please don't hesitate to call," which she didn't really mean at that moment. When alert and rested she enjoyed all aspects of her job. It was hard to be at her best when she needed sleep or food.

Trudging back upstairs she had a hot bath, looked longingly at the book she had read only a few pages from and fell into bed. Grimsby was waiting, he knew that once his mistress had her bath, bedtime was imminent for both of them.

Early the next morning Jennifer awoke to sunshine. Grimsby, who was still lying at the foot of the bed, stretched and yawned and headed for his food dish. She felt well rested and was ready to begin a new day.

She decided that it might be a good day to look for a blue suit. A suit trial might be a good idea before she looked at a winter weight and summer weight option for her staff. Jennifer loved to shop as much as her twin hated it. Her favourite places were second hand and thrift stores although she would shop retail for the suit since it was for work. Many of her leisure clothes were second hand. Shopping was a fun and colourful distraction from the black and grey suits and muted colours of the funeral homes she worked in.

It was still early when she went down to the lounge to make coffee. Elaine would not be in for another hour. In her office she logged on to her computer, read the news, checked her personal email and played a few hands of solitaire. With regular shifts in Toronto, she had time for her computer games at night, she loved her game sites. That had not been the case this week, she had no time to play. She barely had time to catch the headlines and was happy to catch up on the news.

Jennifer heard the front door unlock and rose to greet Elaine, flicking on light switches to get the funeral home ready for the day as she went to the front office.

"Hi Elaine," she said cheerfully.

"Hi to you too. Anything new?

"Just a price shopper last night. I am heading out to the crematorium shortly."

As Elaine started to remove her coat the front door opened. Jennifer turned to see who it was. The man who entered the door did so with purpose. Most people entering a funeral home were hesitant, especially if it was their first time. Not this gentleman. He was on a mission.

"Good morning," said Jennifer, taking in his expensive suit and shoes and noting that he carried himself with military bearing.

"I wish to speak with Ms. Spencer," he stated. It sounded like a command.

"I'm Jennifer Spencer," she said, moving towards him. He towered over her.

"Wisener," he said as a way of introduction. Jennifer extended her hand. His handshake was brief and firm.

"Please, come in Mr. Wisener. May I offer you a coffee or tea?"

"Coffee, black please."

"I'll get it, would like coffee Jennifer?" asked Elaine.

"Tea please Elaine. Thank you."

"Have a seat, Mr. Wisener," said Jennifer as she led him into the office. He settled into one of the wingback chairs beside the desk. Jennifer decided to sit beside him in the other chair rather than behind the desk. He was a bit intimidating and she felt that sitting beside him might make him less so. Course, she thought, sitting behind the desk makes it clear I am in charge, but I suspect it would make very little difference with Mr. Wisener. She hated her moments of insecurity.

"I'd like a better price for this package." Mr. Wisener reached into his suit jacket and pulled out a printed list of some of her services and passed it to her. He obviously had taken careful notes, the prices Jennifer quoted him were exact. She took a minute to scan them. There was no casket or urn listed.

Elaine arrived with the tea and coffee and placed a mug in front of Mr. Wisener, who did not respond.

"Thanks Elaine," said Jennifer. Elaine closed the office door as she left.

Jennifer was puzzled. Not once had Mr. Wisener given her any indication of his intentions. Was there a pending death? Was this a preplanning situation? Why the discount? She picked up her tea and sipped slowly, giving herself a few seconds to plan her approach to his request.

Putting her cup down she raised her head and looked directly at him. Giving him the sense of control he felt he needed, she decided to answer his demand rather than ask questions.

"You have thought this through carefully Mr. Wisener," she said. "In the event we proceed with these arrangements I will consider removing the cost of the trip to pick up the cremated remains if I combine it with another pickup."

Mr. Wisener showed no response whatsoever. He reached for his coffee and sat back in the chair.

The silence lingered.

As he finished his coffee he put his cup down. "I would like to see your facilities now," he stated.

Jennifer nodded and rose to open the door. She led him through the chapel to the suites. He stood in the doorway of each suite taking in every detail. He looked both ways down the hallway and looked at Jennifer.

"The lounge is this way Mr. Wisener," she said as she led the way. Again he stopped at the door. Elaine was sitting talking to Peter, who had popped in for coffee. He was in jeans and neatly dressed. Mr. Wisener looked at her employees.

"Peter, this is Mr. Wisener," said Jennifer. Peter rose, strode across the room and shook his hand.

"Pleased to meet you sir," said Peter.

Mr. Wisener nodded and without a word, turned and strode towards the front door. Jennifer looked at her two employees and made an "I don't have a clue what's going on" face. She found Mr. Wisener standing at the front window looking out. She saw an Audi SUV with a man sitting in the driver's seat.

"Would you like to see our selection room?" asked Jennifer.

"Yes."

No closer to understanding why Mr. Wisener was there, she stuck with her original plan to let him lead the discussion. Once in the selection room she oriented him briefly to the cremation options and started to withdraw.

"Wait Ms. Spencer," said Mr. Wisener. The crisp, commanding tone he had used in the previous conversation was gone.

Jennifer moved back beside him. He looked at the caskets and urns in total silence.

"My son is dying," he said.

Jennifer felt a rush of empathy for him. "I'm so sorry," she said softly.

Mr. Wisener turned to look at her. "I do believe you are," he said. Gone was the no nonsense businessman. His face for that moment was that of a grieving father.

"I will be pulling him off life support when I leave here," he continued.

Walking over to the most expensive wood casket in the room, he put his hand on it. "I will take this one." He approached the urns. There was a hand carved jade urn that had been in the selection room for a long time, a purchase that Uncle Bill had made on a whim years ago. Jennifer had doubted that it would ever sell, it was beautiful but quite costly.

"And this." Mr. Wisener picked up the heavy urn from the top shelf, studied it and handed it to Jennifer. Other than dusting it, Jennifer had not taken it off the shelf. Certain cultures considered jade the "Stone of Heaven". Jennifer wondered if Mr.

Wisener chose on the basis of cost or meaning or both.

For a moment the air between the two of them was heavy with grief. Without another word, Mr. Wisener left the room. Jennifer followed with the urn, which she placed on a table in the hallway and hurried to catch up.

This time he extended his hand. Jennifer responded by taking his hand in both hers, albeit briefly since she understood that his nature did not allow for demonstrative responses.

"Call this number when the contract is ready and I will sign and return it." As Jennifer took his card he opened the door and left.

Heading to the window she discretely watched as a smartly dressed man in a suit opened the back door of the Audi SUV. She had a feeling that a member of his staff would be taking care of things from this point on.

She glanced down at the business card. J.T. Wisener, no first name. The company name, however, did cause her to raise an eyebrow. Heading to the office she looked him up. Mr. Wisener was the CEO and owner of a group of companies based in major cities around the world. He sat on numerous boards and was well known as a philanthropist.

It wasn't about the money, thought Jennifer as she sat back in her chair. Was it about the discretion?

distance? service? He lives in Toronto she thought. Why come here?

She clicked off the search window and tucked his card into her pocket. It took a few minutes to complete the contract which she printed before heading to the lounge. Peter and Elaine were talking quietly. They both looked up as she entered.

"Does the name J.T. Wisener mean anything to you?" asked Jennifer.

Elaine shook her head no. Peter, however, was wide-eyed.

"He's a tech giant, among other things," he responded. "He's worth millions."

Jennifer sat down across from the two of them. "The gentleman who was just here, J.T. Wisener, has a pending death; his son. He prearranged and the death is imminent."

Peter exhaled with a whoosh.

"You and I Peter, will be transferring his son from Toronto. I have no idea why he came to our funeral home, he had his reasons. I know I don't have to say this, but I would rather you not share this information with anyone, not even your spouses or family. It stays between the three of us."

"Understood," said Peter, as Elaine nodded.

"Elaine, will you call the number on the contract to tell whoever answers that the contract is ready?"

"Of course."

"Then I'll be off to take the baby to the crematorium," said Jennifer. "Call me on my cell if you need me."

Jennifer checked her hair in one of the mirrors in the hallway, plucked the keys from the rack in the garage and went to the lead car. On the drive to the crematorium her heart was heavy as she thought about Mr. Wisener, and Matt and Amber, forever changed by the loss of their sons.

6

Later that evening, with the contract signed and returned, Jennifer put away the blue suit she had purchased that afternoon and played with Grimsby, who hunted and attacked his squeaky mouse. Out of the corner of her eye she saw the funeral home line flash. A tiny flash of fear swept through her as she wondered if it was Mr. Wisener. She immediately chided herself for her anxiety. What is the worst that can happen? she told herself. If Mr. Wisener wasn't happy, he could change his mind and go to another funeral home. On the other hand, his son might have died and was calling to report his death.

Why am I so insecure? she thought. I always imagine the worst. I did my best. I'm not perfect but I did my best. Grimsby dropped his mouse at her side and she tossed it across the room. Grimsby leapt to catch it before it stopped. She rose and went to the kitchen to make herself a cup of tea. Too keyed up to sit, she stood at the counter waiting to see if the answering service was going to call. She knew that if the death had occurred the answering service would put the caller right through and if it was an inquiry they would take the caller's information and call her on her cell.

Her cell rang. Breathing slowly to calm her nerves, she answered. It was an inquiry and Jennifer took the information, annoyed with herself at her weakness.

She called the family back, taking time to let them ask questions. They set up an appointment for later the next day.

Finishing her tea, she then ran a bath. As she lay back in the bubbles with her eyes closed she heard her cell go off. Scrambling out of the tub and grabbing a towel she made it on the fourth ring. The answering service told her they had Dr. Gibson from a hospital in Toronto on the line and put him through.

"Ms. Spencer—Dr. Gibson at Toronto General Hospital. Aaron Wisener died a few minutes ago. I understand you will be coming from out of town. Don't rush, when you arrive at the admitting department, please ask for me and I will meet you."

"We will be on the road within the half hour. Thank you Dr. Gibson."

Jennifer dialed Peter, told him they'd be going to Toronto, asked him to wear his funeral suit and suggested she pick him up. She scrambled to get dressed and headed to the door. She paused for a minute, turned around and scooped up Grimsby, who started purring.

"Thanks buddy," she said, stroking him gently. "You keep me grounded." She put him down, gave him a treat and left her apartment less than ten minutes after Dr. Gibson's call.

She doubled checked the van supplies, made sure she had her Tim's card so they could get coffee and opened the garage door. As she pulled out, she thought she caught a glimpse of someone in her headlights. Spooked, she hit the garage door closer and put her brights on, driving slowly through the parking lot looking to see if it could be an intruder. Not seeing anyone or any movement, she continued through the lot, onto the side street, scanning carefully. Nothing. As an added precaution she circled the funeral home one more time just to be sure. There were cars parked on the street and as she drove by, she checked to see if anyone was sitting inside them. If someone had been lurking, they were gone. The new lock can't come soon enough she thought, as she turned off her brights and headed to Peter's. He was waiting on his porch as she pulled up.

"Hey Peter. Ready for a coffee?"

"You bet," he replied. "I can run in."

Tim's was a few blocks from his house. Jennifer parked on the street and Peter walked in. Even at that hour of the night it was busy. As she waited, she wondered if Travis was behind the break-in and if the cash in the casket had something to do with him. He had returned his keys to the funeral home but there was no reason why he didn't keep one of the spares. She made a mental note to count the spare garage door keys. Each key was marked "Do Not Duplicate" but that didn't mean in the wrong hands it couldn't be done. She thought about asking the police if they had an idea what might be going on.

Peter returned to the van with doughnuts and coffee. It was a pleasant drive to Toronto; the highways were not too busy at that hour and Jennifer knew the quickest route through the city.

The front of the hospital was quiet in the still of the night. Jennifer chose to drop Peter off at the front door to go to the admitting department and ask for Dr. Gibson. She drove the van to the back and waited for them to unlock the morgue bay door. This hospital had a garage for privacy, one of the few in the city.

She drove around to the back of the hospital, collected the coffee cups and garbage and tossed them in the dumpster while she waited for Peter and their escort. She more or less knew her way from the pathology department to admitting but thought it might be best to ask Dr. Gibson if they could have a security guard escort them from the floor back to the morgue bay. Removing a deceased person from a hospital room was not normal procedure and the last thing she and Peter wanted was to get lost wandering in endless hallways trying to find their way back to the van.

Standing on the loading dock watching the trucks being unloaded reminded her of her time in Toronto. That chapter in her life was over, she thought, the frenetic bustle of the city was no longer part of her daily routine. Once more she felt thankful and grateful for the turn her life had taken.

Fifteen minutes passed before she heard a door open behind her. Peter and a gentleman in a suit stood in the bay. Jennifer walked toward them.

"Jennifer, this is Dr. Gibson," said Peter.

"Ms. Spencer, nice to meet you," said Dr. Gibson with a nod. "Trust you had a good trip. I'm going to direct you to another entrance if you don't mind."

Peter was standing slightly behind Dr. Gibson and gave a slight shrug and a look that confirmed he didn't know what was happening either. Dr. Gibson walked outside and climbed into the passenger side of the van, hitting the door closer as he left the bay. Peter followed and quietly told Jennifer he would get into the back. Jennifer was momentarily puzzled. Standard protocol meant removing deceased persons through the morgue bay. Obviously, this isn't the case this time, she thought. Interesting.

Peter was discretely as he climbed into the back of the van where he crouched beside the stretcher. It didn't look comfortable.

"Are you OK?" she asked.

"I'm fine." He gave her a smile. She closed the van door behind him and climbed into the driver's seat beside Dr. Gibson.

"Go to the west side of the building, I'll direct you through the security gate."

Jennifer oriented herself quickly and backed up. Dr. Gibson didn't correct her as she drove left and around the corner. Whew, she thought. At least I got west correct.

They drove past several good-sized parking lots on their left before Dr. Gibson spoke again. "On your right, the gate there." A small set of parking spaces were protected by a lift gate. There were a couple of parked cars and a door into the hospital. Dr. Gibson hit a button on his key fob and the gate rose. "Just back up in here," he said.

Perhaps this is a doctor's entrance, thought Jennifer as she maneuvered the van into place and shut it down.

"Bring the stretcher, we will leave it in the hallway," said Dr. Gibson as he jumped out. Peter had managed to let himself out and was removing the stretcher as she got to the back of the van. She locked the van as Dr. Gibson opened the door to the hospital into a quiet enclosed room with an elevator. Peter put the stretcher beside the elevator as Dr. Gibson swiped his card for access. The elevator doors opened. It was not your standard hospital elevator, it looked more like it belonged in a luxury hotel.

"I expect you have not used this entrance before Ms. Spencer?" asked Dr. Gibson with a smile.

"Never. And I have been to this hospital many times."

"Certain patients require discretion," said Dr. Gibson. "This affords the privacy they need."

Or can afford, thought Jennifer as they boarded. The elevator rose swiftly and silently up. There were no numbered buttons, it went to one destination.

With a soft swoosh the door opened to quiet luxury. Jennifer and Peter glanced around. Floor to ceiling windows overlooked the lights of the city. Elegant tables with lamps and beautiful flower arrangements, and comfortable seating were placed to maximize the view.

"Wow," said Peter softly. Dr. Gibson gave them a few minutes to take in their surroundings.

"One never gets used to the view," he said. "It is magnificent, isn't it?"

Leading them to a paneled oak door, he swiped

his card again. "This will give us direct access to Aaron's room. There are two patient rooms on this floor, each with their own access."

Aaron's room was a suite and again Jennifer and Peter did their best not to react to the luxury, cognizant of their role and the reason they were there. While Jennifer had worked with wealthy clients and transferred bodies from mansions once or twice, this was an experience she suspected very few funeral directors would ever get.

It was as if Dr. Gibson had read her mind. "Normally we do transfer deceased individuals to the morgue," he said. "Occasionally there are exceptions. Mr. Wisener is our largest benefactor."

He led the way through living area. TV, faux fireplace, dining room, all with a view, thought Jennifer. Not one bit of it was clinical or resembled a hospital room. Passing through a short hallway they entered Aaron's room. A woman rose as Dr. Gibson entered. She was wearing a business suit. Her name tag said Monica Godwin RN.

"Hello Monica."

"Hi Dr. Gibson. Shall I return in a few minutes?"

"Please," said Dr. Gibson and Monica disappeared.

Aaron's body was covered with a sheet. Jennifer could tell immediately that it wasn't the standard hospital issue. The medical equipment that she was used to seeing was not in sight and she suspected that it had been removed once life support had been withdrawn. There was a table with chairs that resembled a board room setting close to the window and Dr. Gibson led them there.

"Have a seat," he said. Peter and Jennifer sat down, glancing over the city vista quickly before turning their attention to Dr. Gibson.

He opened the leather folder sitting on the table and leaned back in his chair.

"We have arranged for you to have an escort out of the city, they will drop off once you are in the Niagara region. Mr. Wisener wants to ensure that no one follows you. When you are about fifteen minutes away from the funeral home, please call this number. You will see an unmarked vehicle at the funeral home, just proceed as normal." He handed the phone number to Peter. "They will remain in the parking lot all day tomorrow as well."

Jennifer knew that Mr. Wisener did not want an obituary, that had not been part of his list. She had not offered it or questioned him about it. Clearly he required discretion but an escort? That raised things a notch.

"I can assume you will be proceeding to the crematorium first thing in the morning the day after tomorrow?"

"Yes," responded Jennifer.

"The security team will accompany you and Peter to the crematorium."

"Understood," responded Jennifer. Normally she or Peter would make the trip by themselves but the *you and Peter* made it clear that would not be the case this time. She realized that dropping Peter off at his home on the way back would not be an option either, he would have to take a cab home. She considered giving him the lead car for the night but thought better of it.

"Here is the death certificate," said Dr. Gibson as he handed her an envelope. She slipped it into the inside pocket of her funeral jacket.

"Finally," said Dr. Gibson. "The clothing Aaron is wearing now is to stay on."

Jennifer raised an eyebrow.

"It's OK Ms. Spencer. There are no metal objects or medical paraphernalia that could damage the retort. Of course we expect you to check, that is your job. But we did ensure that nothing impeded cremation. Any questions or concerns?" he added.

"How is Mr. Wisener?" asked Jennifer. For a second Dr. Gibson looked sad.

"Mr. Wisener has been my friend for many years and he is, like any father, deeply grieving." Jennifer was starting to understand why the doctor had met them and why he had passed on Mr.

Wisener's wishes. It was unusual to have a physician pass on information in the manner that Dr. Gibson had. Clearly Mr. Wisener trusted his old friend.

Monica entered the room.

"Peter, would you mind going with Monica to get your stretcher?" asked Dr. Gibson.

Peter rose and left with Monica. The room was silent and still and Jennifer felt the presence of death. Dr. Gibson seemed pensive, as if he felt it too. She stared out at the city for a few seconds then turned to Dr. Gibson.

"Thank you for your assistance and understanding," she said. "This was a much different scenario than what we are used to and you made it as comfortable as possible."

Dr. Gibson smile was warm. "It was my pleasure."

As Peter and Monica entered the room with the stretcher, he rose.

"Would you like some help?" he asked.

"We should be OK thanks," responded Jennifer and she and Peter prepared to transfer Aaron to the stretcher. Jennifer had placed gloves in the pouch and she and Peter donned them, lowered the stretcher to the height of the bed and slid Aaron's body onto the pouch. Jennifer tucked the folded sheets she had on the stretcher under Aaron's head. Monica and Dr. Gibson stood quietly by as Jennifer closed the zipper.

Normally she and Peter would remove their gloves and place them in the pouch but this time she chose not to, recognizing that Monica would ensure disposal. Peter had intuitively followed his bosses lead. Monica picked up a nearby container, Jennifer and Peter stripped off their gloves, dropped them into the outstretched container and quietly left the room.

Monica swiped her key for the elevator. "Take care," she said as the doors opened.

"Thank you, you too," said Jennifer. She and Peter rode to the first floor in silence. Once outside Peter loaded the stretcher as Jennifer looked around for their escort. They were nowhere to be seen.

Peter came around the side of the vehicle. "I think we might want to keep our conversation to a minimum," he said quietly. "Security firms at this level can eavesdrop in strange places." Jennifer nodded.

"Would you like to drive?" she asked Peter.

"Sure," was the response. The gate rose as Peter started the van. Jennifer and Peter kept glancing in the side mirrors to see if there was a car following them. If there was, it was keeping a discreet distance in the city. As they entered the feeder lanes for the drive outside Toronto there was no way to tell if they had an escort; the traffic was heavy, as it often was

112

on the highway.

"How's Angel?" asked Jennifer.

"Good. She, I mean we, got some good news today."

Jennifer glanced over at Peter. He was smiling.

"She's pregnant."

"Oh Peter, that's great news! When is she due?"

"It's early. We think she's six weeks along."

"I'm so happy for you."

They spent the next while discussing Peter's family. Finally, Jennifer spoke up.

"I have news too—Marcia will be joining the firm soon."

"I really like Marcia. You two make a great team. It should make your workload a lot easier." He paused. "Where is she going to live?"

"Not sure yet. The decision was just made. Knowing Marcia, she'll look for a condo in Niagara Falls. Course, my aunt and uncle's cottage might be an option, it's less than 1/2 hour away from the funeral home and it's on Lake Erie. I haven't been down yet to check it out yet."

Once they saw the sign for Niagara, Jennifer relaxed a bit. The escort should have dropped off.

"We should be back home in about forty minutes. I was going to drop you off but that would probably not be a good idea. Are you OK taking a cab home?" asked Jennifer.

"Absolutely. What time do you want me tomorrow?"

"Elaine will be in at 9 a.m., how does 9:15 sound? That should give you about seven hours sleep if you're lucky."

Peter laughed. "I'm a parent," he said. "Sleep? What's that? Can I buy or borrow some?"

Jennifer responded in kind. "I'm a funeral director. Sleep? You're asking the wrong person—I have no idea."

Twenty minutes away from the funeral home Jennifer checked her phone. "Guess I should make that call now," she said.

"Oh—right," said Peter as he reached into his pocket for the number.

Jennifer checked her cell phone signal, put her phone on speaker, and dialed the number Dr. Gibson had given Peter. A quick ring and an automated tone responded with two beeps. The call disconnected by itself before she could say hello. She and Peter glanced at each other, itching to discuss what had been happening. There would be time to talk about the experience later.

"Would you be able to give me a few minutes of your time when we get back?" asked Jennifer. Peter picked up what she meant, that she wanted to casket Aaron.

"Of course."

Pulling into the funeral home lot Jennifer and Peter spotted a van tucked into the corner of the lot. Jennifer hit the garage door opener and Peter backed in before closing the door to the outside world. Once Jennifer had double checked to ensure Aaron was ready for cremation, she and Peter casketed him. The medical certificate indicated Aaron had suffered a head injury secondary to a fall on a ski slope. She made a mental note to see if there was anything about his accident archived in the news and she wondered why she hadn't seen a mention of it in her Googling of Wisener earlier. Aaron was only 24 years old, two years younger than she was, and it saddened her.

The next morning came too quickly. Grimsby jumped off the bed once his mistress stirred, ready to start his day with breakfast. Jennifer was too nauseated from the lack of sleep to eat. Maybe I'll have time this afternoon to sneak in a nap, she thought. The visitation could be busy.

She took a peek out of her window. The van was still there. Once Peter arrived she would send him to City Hall for the burial permit for Aaron's cremation. She and Elaine would ensure the suite and funeral home were spotless.

Mid-morning a florist van pulled in. By the time Peter had returned with the permit, most of the cleaning was done. The flower van pulled up to the garage door, and the florist walked around to the front and asked to be let in. Jennifer had not seen that company before so she checked quickly on the computer in her office. The florist was from Toronto.

When the florist opened the van door they were caught off guard. The flowers were magnificent white and brown roses. The florist proudly explained that they were Osiria roses, a rare variety. Several hundred of them were in the casket spray alone, dozens more in the two large arrangements. Carefully she and Peter and the florist carried the spray into the suite and placed the heavy flowers on Aaron's casket. Once the side arrangements were in place, the suite had been transformed.

"It's breathtaking," said Elaine in awe.

"I have never seen such a rose, let alone heard of Osirias before," said Peter.

"Me either," said Jennifer. She made a mental note to take a close up of one of the roses with her phone later. The fragrance coming from the roses was heavenly.

She sent Peter home for the afternoon after lunch, met with the latest family with a pending death, then told Elaine to call her in a few hours or sooner if needed and then went upstairs to nap. Jennifer was going to order in supper for the three of them. Once Jennifer was upstairs, Grimsby dropped his squeaky toy at her feet, she tossed it for him a few times, hung up her suit and crawled under her duvet. Within minutes she was sound asleep.

Three hours later she awoke refreshed and ready for the evening. She redid her hair and make-up and went downstairs, placing her high heels on the stairs for later. She went into the suite and took a close up of one of the roses with her phone. Elaine was reading a book in the office. She joined Jennifer for tea in the lounge and they discussed Marcia's pending move. Jennifer suggested that Marcia might be comfortable in the cottage for the summer if she wanted time to look for a condo. She and Elaine decided to take a drive to the lake over the next few days to check it out.

Once Peter arrived, Jennifer ordered supper for them and over dinner the three discussed everything but the visitation that evening. They were prepared for a large crowd but unsure of what to expect. There had been no death notice in any of the major papers.

"Peter, you're the social media expert. Why do you suppose there was no mention of Aaron's accident in the media? I did a quick check, I didn't see anything," said Jennifer. Peter pulled out his phone.

It took him less than two minutes to find it.

"Aaron was injured in Switzerland about ten days ago, a skiing accident." He handed Jennifer the phone and she read the brief report, passing to Elaine. Getting Aaron back to Canada and placing him under Dr. Gibson's care must have been difficult for Mr. Wisener.

After dinner Jennifer went outside and walked around the funeral home checking the parking lot for garbage. She tried not to look at the van in the corner of the lot, but couldn't resist, giving them a tiny wave as she walked over to the dumpster with the little bit of litter she had collected. There was no response, not that she expected one.

Back in her office, she called Marcia, talking to her about her pending move. Marcia had given her notice and would be starting within the month. She was quite open to the idea of living in the cottage for the summer if she wasn't able to find a place in time. She and Phil were also planning to come down for their trip to the casino for dinner and a show. They set a date six days away; Jennifer would book the show. Peter was surfing on the computer in the office and Elaine was reading.

By 6:50 p.m. not one car was in the lot. It wasn't unusual to have just family attend a visitation but the only family Jennifer was aware of was Mr. Wisener.

At 7 p.m. sharp Mr. Wisener's Audi SUV pulled up to the front of the funeral home. The driver let Mr. Wisener out. Jennifer met him at the door.

"Hello Mr. Wisener."

He nodded. "Ms. Spencer."

She held his gaze for a brief second, then said, "This way please," and led him down the hall to the suite.

He paused at the door, looked around the suite then turned to Jennifer. "Please close these doors until 9 p.m."

"Of course," Jennifer responded and as quietly as possible slid the pocket doors to the suite shut.

Mr. Wisener's driver was standing at the front door. "Would you be so kind as to lock the funeral home doors? I will return for Mr. Wisener at 9 p.m."

"I will. That is, with the understanding that if another family needs arrangements and comes to the door, I will take them into the office."

"Understood," said the driver as he left. Jennifer complied with the request to lock the door and went to the lounge.

"There will be no visitors," she said to Elaine and Peter. "So you both have the rest of the evening off." As an afterthought, she added, "With pay, of course."

"In that case, see you first thing in the morning," said Peter happily. "Goodnight."

"Goodnight Jennifer," echoed Elaine. The two of them headed for the garage door.

Faced with the next two hours of silence

Jennifer pondered her options. She decided to stay near the front door in the unlikely event someone did need arrangements. She went to the lounge, poured herself a tea and took it to the front office.

The two hours dragged slowly. Jennifer caught up on the funeral journals, played solitaire and backgammon on the computer and read one of her sister's news articles. At 8:30 p.m. she walked quietly down the hall to peek through the crack in the pocket doors. Mr. Wisener was sitting in the wingback chair, not moving. The impact of his grief was palpable and Jennifer's heart ached for him. She returned silently to the office to wait out the remaining time.

At 8:59 p.m. Mr. Wisener's car pulled up. Jennifer watched the driver exit and she unlocked the front door. Precisely at 9 p.m. Mr. Wisener opened the door to the suite and walked to the front entrance.

"Thank you Ms. Spencer," he said as he extended his hand.

Again, Jennifer took his hand briefly in her two, established eye contact and gave his hand a gentle squeeze.

"Take care Mr. Wisener," was all she said. He nodded, his driver opened the door and the two of them disappeared into the night.

Jennifer waited until they pulled away, then shut

down the lounge and the front of the funeral home for the night. When she went to the suite to shut off the lights she noticed a single rose from the arrangements lying on the arm of the chair. Picking it up, she marvelled at the delicacy of the colour and its perfection, and inhaled the rare fragrance. She decided to take it upstairs with her, preserve it in her convection oven, then spray it with floral sealant. She would wrap it in cellophane and return it to Mr. Wisener when the urn was picked up.

She lingered in the solemn silence of the suite for a few minutes then turned, shut off the lights and went upstairs.

7

The next morning Peter arrived early to take Aaron to the crematorium with Jennifer. As they left the funeral home they watched to see if the van in the corner of the parking lot was going to follow them, but that didn't appear to be the case. Once at the crematorium, the operator, Donnie, met them.

"We'll call you later today when the cremation is completed," he said.

"Thanks Donnie," responded Jennifer. "Appreciate it." She handed Donnie the paperwork and the urn, which she had placed in its wooden box.

"That's a nice piece of jade," said Donnie as he opened the box. "Don't see too many of those."

"No. Uncle Bill bought that on a whim many years ago."

"Your Uncle told me about that purchase, it was a little steep," chuckled Donnie. "He said the stone almost spoke to him."

"It was steep, so it wasn't the money talking," said Jennifer with a smile. "Thanks Donnie, see you later today."

Back at the funeral home, Jennifer and Peter noticed there was a car parked at the side of the building. Elaine met her as she came down the hall.

"Detective Sergeant Gillespie would like to talk to you," she said.

"Did he say why?" asked Jennifer in a low voice. Elaine shook her head.

"Not a word. He just arrived. I got him a coffee. Want one?"

"Please," said Jennifer as she headed to the office.

"Hello Detective Sergeant," she said brightly. "What can I do for you?"

"Hello Ms. Spencer. I have some information."

Jennifer cocked her head. "I'm listening."

Elaine entered the office and handed Jennifer her coffee. "Peter was wondering if he should stay until you hear from the crematorium?" she asked.

"If he wants to. They should be calling in a couple of hours."

"And, the family who was here yesterday would like you to call, they have a few questions for you. I told them you would get back to them by noon."

"Thanks." Elaine disappeared down the hall.

Jennifer turned back to her unexpected visitor.

"We got a call from a security firm that someone tried to enter the funeral home last night. Apparently the security firm scared him off."

Jennifer caught her breath. She stared at Detective Sergeant Gillespie, at a loss for words.

"They reported that he drove off in a Taurus," he continued.

"Travis?" said Jennifer in a shaky voice.

"Possibly. Until we know why this individual is attempting to enter and who he is I would suggest you take extra precautions. In the event you have a call in the middle of the night, please ensure you have a partner. Make sure you latch the garage door when you close up at night."

"The new lock will be here in a few days."

"Nonetheless, I want you to take this seriously. The new lock may not be a deterrent and until we know who is responsible, please be careful." He finished his coffee and stood. Jennifer remained in her chair, not trusting herself to get up. All the questions she had wanted to ask the police were forgotten.

Detective Sergeant Gillespie dropped a card on the desk. "Call this number immediately if you hear something suspicious or if you're going out at night."

He exited the office without another word. A few minutes later Jennifer found her legs and went to the lounge to tell Peter and Elaine. She wanted to be sure that her staff was safe. They all agreed to be especially careful. Peter reassured Jennifer that he would ensure they were always aware of where each other was and that no one would leave the funeral home alone.

Jennifer then returned the call from the family who had prearranged, then Peter and Jennifer discussed the security team that had been in place. Peter explained that technology such as parabolic mics made it possible for the security team to hear what conversations took place in the vehicles and monitor their indoor conversation. "The same probably held true for the funeral home while Mr. Wisener was here," said Peter. "And I suspect they know who tried to break in last night. A security firm as technically advanced as that one has the latest technology and access to information the police may not readily have."

"Do you suspect it had something to do with Mr. Wisener?" asked Jennifer.

"Dunno. If it was a coincidence it was a fortunate one. They can track a person down pretty quickly. I'm sure Mr. Wisener has his share of enemies. He has people whose job it is to keep personal information out of the press, and his security firm to ensure he isn't followed." Or it might have something to do with the cash in the casket, thought Jennifer.

Peter offered to wash the vehicles and Jennifer

and Elaine took care of some administrative duties over the next hour. She then called to book the show tickets for the following week, smiling to herself at the thought of the fun she and Marcia and Phil always had on their nights out.

When the crematorium called to say they could come to pick up the urn, Jennifer and Peter took the lead car this time and, as they exited the garage, she nodded at the security van to let them know they were ready for the escort. Once again the escort was discrete.

Back at the funeral home, Jennifer called the number Mr. Wisener had given her. A pleasant receptionist explained that a driver would be there shortly to pick up the urn. She finalized the bill, giving Mr. Wisener the discount even though she had made an exclusive trip to the crematorium. She wasn't quite sure why she chose to discount the crematorium trip. Perhaps it was because Mr. Wisener's security team kept the intruder out, and she was grateful for the help. *It isn't always about money* her Uncle Bill would often say and Jennifer agreed. She had hated billing families for every little detail when she worked for the corporate funeral home. Now she had the option to use her discretion and it just felt right.

Twenty minutes later the front door opened and the same driver who had accompanied Mr. Wisener both times walked in. He must be staying in the area, thought Jennifer. Maybe Mr. Wisener has several drivers. She rose to meet him.

"Good afternoon," she said. "Please come in." She led the way to the office.

"Good afternoon Ms. Spencer," said the driver. He watched as Jennifer placed the urn box in the velvet urn bag and pulled the drawstring.

"I saved a rose from the arrangement," she explained as she handed him the wrapped flower she had preserved.

"That was very thoughtful," said the driver as she handed him an envelope with paperwork and proceeded to put the completed invoice in a separate envelope.

"No need to seal it," said the driver as he pulled it out of the envelope. He scanned it quickly, pulled out his phone and sent a text, then returned the invoice to the envelope.

"I, that is, well, I wanted to thank Mr. Wisener's security team for stopping the intruder," Jennifer stammered. The driver smiled warmly at her.

"Glad they could help," he said. His phone chimed and he glanced down at it.

"Your services have been paid in full," said the driver as he pocketed his phone and stood to leave. Jennifer marvelled at how efficient Mr. Wisener's world seemed to be. Of course, his people would know how to direct deposit to the funeral home account even if she hadn't given them the information.

"Thank you. I don't think I will ever forget Mr. Wisener," said Jennifer as she walked the driver to the door. "He was a true gentleman and he suffered such a terrible loss."

As Jennifer opened the door for Mr. Wisener's driver he paused and pulled an envelope from his pocket. "He asked me to give you this," he said as he handed it to her. "All the best to you Ms. Spencer."

"And to you too," said Jennifer as he left. She leaned with her back against the door. Like a little kid she wanted to just slide to the floor and have a good cry.

The past few days had tested her and while she was proud of the way she and her staff had handled the Wisener call from beginning to end, she wasn't happy with her initial judgement of the man. That will teach me not to second guess a caller, she told herself. He wasn't shopping, he was grieving and he needed some control. Even if he was shopping around that was his right. Lesson learned.

She looked at the envelope the driver had given her. Heading back to the office she sat in the wingback chair and opened it. It was handwritten on embossed white stationary.

My dear Ms. Spencer, the letter started. Jennifer

was touched by the formality of his writing. She continued to read.

I had not understood how hard it would be to lose someone I loved.

You have found your calling. I cannot thank you enough for your empathy and support.

John Wisener.

Jennifer went upstairs, greeted Grimsby and put the letter in her keepsake box.

8

I need a haircut, what is the name of your hairdresser again? Jennifer texted to Gwen. Seconds later Gwen replied with *Marco* and the phone number for the salon. A minute later she followed with, *I have an appointment this Thursday at 9 a.m. do you want me to see if he can take you at 9:30?*

Please, I'll buy the lattes, responded Jennifer.

Ten minutes later Gwen confirmed the appointment. Jennifer had been going to the same hairdresser in Toronto for years and was ready for a change. At the corporate funeral home with regular hours she had time to fuss over her looks. She was quickly learning that it might be time for a shorter, easier to care for cut, most of her days were at least ten hours long.

The next few days were busy, she had a few more calls. One funeral service had been held in the chapel, the other at a church. When she had gone to pick up the coach at Williams Funeral Home for the church funeral, the owner, Dimitri asked if she could assist in the event they had more than two calls: he was going to be away for a week and the new director he hired recently was still finding his way around.

Dimitri looked haggard and distracted. Jennifer was happy to help. He and Uncle Bill had been good friends and covered for each other for vacations and days off. Dimitri introduced her to the new director, Drew, a recent graduate. She reassured him that she would be happy to assist, and to call at any time. The obvious relief on Drew's face was thanks enough.

Jennifer had started wearing her blue suit and rather liked it. She was excited when she woke Thursday morning, having spent the previous evening pouring over hairstyles online. She texted Gwen around 7:30 a.m. to tell her she would take her out for a latte before they got their cuts. Gwen usually didn't eat breakfast coming off her shifts, she preferred something light.

Half an hour later they were tucked into a booth at Tim's chattering about work. Gwen mentioned that things had been going well. The dealer she thought might have been under suspicion was still working and the job wasn't quite as stressful, the new pit boss adhered to policy.

"How are the kids?" asked Jennifer.

"Ha," said Gwen. "My daughter has decided she has had enough of kindergarten. She announced it was for babies and she wanted to go to Grade 3 now."

Jennifer laughed. "I don't know about you, but in the school I attended, the Grade 3 kids seemed so grown up and they went to a classroom upstairs. We kindergarteners were not allowed to climb the stairs."

Gwen nodded. "The only thing I remember about kindergarten was the red-headed boy who gave me dandelions. We held hands during recess. His name was Dennis."

Finishing their lattes, the two of them headed to the salon. Gwen was greeted by a handsome Italian man who acted like a perfect gentleman. Jennifer sat in the waiting room and watched. He didn't flirt, he didn't gossip, he listened to Gwen's chatter and laughed at her jokes, his scissors and comb flying.

When Marco completed Gwen's cut he flung off her cape with a flourish. Gwen made a crack about messing it all up because she was heading home to bed.

"Do you mind if I call it a night?" Gwen asked Jennifer.

"Not at all. Thanks for meeting me for lattes and making the appointment."

Marco took his time to find out her likes and dislikes. He kept the small talk to a minimum, letting Jennifer take the lead. Jennifer was happy just to sit and feel pampered. She watched her long hair become shorter and didn't mind a bit; she was excited to make the change.

When Marco finished, she surveyed the results with pleasure. She loved her new haircut, it was a short stylish bob and easy to care for. With Marcia and Phil coming down tomorrow for a night in the Falls, they would be picking her up and she could get Phil's opinion about the suit and her haircut, as well as show him around the funeral home. She was looking forward to seeing them both.

She checked her phone as she left the salon. Elaine had not called or texted so Jennifer took a few minutes to shop for a pair of blue pumps to match the new suit. The rest of the day was uneventful and quiet. Jennifer used the time to look at taking some online courses. She registered for a bookkeeping course wondering if she would be happier in a classroom. The online course could be taken at her leisure and a classroom course, while more interesting and social, meant missing classes if she had a call.

She and Elaine went to the cottage after work. It was Jennifer's first visit and she was pleasantly surprised. It was a quaint two bedroom on Lake Erie with a long laneway, placing it well off the highway. Mr. Duncan had arranged for a maintenance crew to care for the lawn and flowers, and Jennifer was pleased to see how tidy it looked. She had considered selling the property; Anne had been reticent. Anne enjoyed being alone, she loved being near water and wanted to keep the cottage. They had discussed renting it out and Anne had agreed to take care of those details. Marcia had been looking for a condo in the Falls, she had some good leads and was planning on staying at the cottage until she found the right place. Anne had already rented the cottage out for late summer and into the fall, the rental income covered all the outdoor maintenance and taxes with plenty left over for cleaning staff between tourists. Jennifer was sure she could do some of the cleaning herself if she didn't have any calls, it would add to the savings.

Upon entering the cottage, Jennifer immediately felt Uncle Bill and Aunt Jean's presence. Aunt Jean's touches were obvious in her colour choices and decorations. A chair by the window overlooking the lake was clearly Uncle Bill's, a newspaper dated six months before he died rested on the side table. A screened-in front porch had a table and chairs overlooking the lake. The tidy bedrooms needed some updated linens, the bathroom also needed some sprucing up.

As Elaine measured the rooms, Jennifer walked out the screened porch toward the lake, overcome with emotion. She was so grateful for the kindness of her aunt and uncle, they had given her so much love growing up, and to have the funeral home and the cottage was almost more than she could bear. As she stood on the shore watching the waves lap the sand, she again realized how much she missed them.

Elaine was clearly enthused by the cottage and the decorating opportunity, so Jennifer gladly turned it over to her. Elaine had good taste and was eager to start working on getting the cottage ready for Marcia and future tenants.

"Why don't you and your husband stay here for a week?" Jennifer suggested. "You can come back to the funeral home as needed."

"Are you sure?" Elaine exclaimed.

Jennifer nodded. "I'm turning you loose with the budget. Enjoy."

On the drive back, Elaine busied herself making notes and announced to Jennifer that she expected to have it completed in under a week.

Dimitri left the next day for his week away and had barely been gone a few hours when Drew called. He was unsure how to finish prepping a body for a service the next day and wanted reassurance. Jennifer called Peter to come in for an hour, deciding to drive back to Williams Funeral Home and work with him directly, rather than over the phone.

Walking into the back entrance of Williams Funeral Home she could detect cigarette smoke.

Laws in Canada banned smoking in public places, and in Ontario, employees and visitors had to smoke a nine-metre distance away from the building. Clearly one of Dimitri's employees was breaking the rules. When she had located Drew in the prep room she asked him if he smoked.

"No," he said. "Some of the staff do. Jorge was here for a while, he smokes." Jennifer looked at the young director carefully. He appeared to be telling the truth so she brushed it off. Butt out, she told herself, it's not your problem. She grimaced to herself at the play on words.

"So, what can I help you with?" she asked Drew. The next hour was spent reassuring the young man he did know what he was doing, he just needed to build confidence. She coached him while they worked and helped with casketing. Once Drew was confident in his abilities, he would be able to run the funeral home and give Dimitri time off. She let him know he was doing great and to call if he needed her.

Back at her office she looked over the accounts. The call volume had been steady, the types of funerals were varied, they tended to be on the more traditional side. She was able to comfortably pay salaries and overhead. Jennifer was aware that asking Marcia to come and work for her was a smart move, it would add balance to her life, work would not be all consuming. She did not want to burn out like some of the directors she had known, who had to leave funeral service for a less stressful life.

The locksmith called before noon to let her know the new lock on the garage entrance was in. They installed it later that day. Any rogue or stray key that was out there was now void. She would always make sure to latch the door at night as an extra precaution. The overhead door could be opened by remote and the only remotes were inside. Her new world was feeling more secure.

Shortly after the locksmith left, Jennifer immersed herself in the news online. The phone jarred her out of her immersion in an op-ed piece about pending legislation surrounding small business taxation. Jennifer was struggling to understand the article.

"Spencer Funeral Home."

"Ummm, that is, my name is Jordan and I work with a victim support group." Jennifer was aware of such organizations, volunteers who worked with emergency services to provide immediate assistance to victims of crimes, accidents or tragic circumstances. The volunteers would then refer the families to community agencies for ongoing support. The volunteers were well-trained, Jennifer had taken the same training and worked with such an agency for a few years before college.

"Hi Jordan, I'm Jennifer. You're with a family?"

"Ummm, yes, well, we ummm, we were wondering if we could talk to you."

"Is your partner with the family now Jordan?"

"Ummm, no, she had to leave to go home to look after her kids."

"Are you able to talk to me?"

"Yes … yes." He hesitated for a few seconds. "There ma'am, I have walked away a bit. My partner and I were working with this family whose son committed suicide, they need some advice."

Jennifer felt for him. There was a reason why volunteers worked in teams, he was on his own and this situation was challenging.

"There was a death by suicide?" she prompted.

The term *commit suicide* was a throwback to the Middle Ages when it was considered criminal and sinful to kill oneself. The term *commit* still implied that a crime was committed. Jennifer knew he had been trained to use the correct terminology, he'd just forgotten.

"Yes," responded Jordan with some emphasis as he remembered his training.

"What do you and the family need from me?"

"Well, could we, that is, are you open? They need some advice as to what to do next."

"I would be pleased to meet with the family. Will you be coming too?"

Jordan hesitated. Jennifer suspected he wanted nothing more than to turn the family over to someone else.

She continued. "Let me just make it clear, I will meet with the family and give them their options. They will make the decision as to what funeral home they want to use and how they wish to proceed. I will also provide them with some resources for the future, knowing that they will not want to look at them at this point in time, but might utilize them later."

She could hear Jordan exhale.

"Alright ma'am, I'll bring them over."

"OK Jordan, I'll see you in a bit." Jennifer hung up and went to gather some material for survivors of suicide loss and a few other documents.

When the family entered the funeral home they stood at the entrance. They didn't look around, they didn't speak, they just stood there. Jennifer sized up the group quickly. There was a slightly older couple, probably the parents. There were three other people, younger, possibly siblings. There was also a young man in a bright shirt who held the door open for them.

Must be Jordan, she thought, as she approached the group. Their grief was palpable, weighing down even the air itself. It was like a wall surrounding the little group, impenetrable and solid.

140

Jennifer stood in front of the family and folded her hands in front of her. She did not attempt to shake their hands or overwhelm them with a greeting. She paused for a few seconds.

"My name is Jennifer," she said. "Jordan explained to me that you lost a family member to suicide today."

No one responded. Only one family member looked at her and the look was bordering on hostile. She didn't really expect them to answer. Again she paused, the silence heavy.

"Let's go sit and talk. This way."

She looked at Jordan, knowing that he had the rapport with the family and should be the one to lead. He stepped forward and Jennifer turned slowly, dropped her hands to her side and took them to the lounge.

The family followed in silence and, shuffling into the lounge, took a seat at a conversation grouping Jennifer had set up for them. Jennifer asked Jordan to pull up a few more club chairs. He complied.

"Ma'am," said Jordan. "May I speak with you?"

Jennifer took him aside and waited for him to speak.

"I don't know what to do now."

"You don't have to stay Jordan," said Jennifer quietly. "I will make sure the family gets home when we are done. But you are welcome to stay."

"It's just that I don't know what to say," he said miserably.

Jennifer touched his arm firmly. "You don't have to say anything. Your presence alone is support enough for them. Right now, in their shock and grief, they won't hear much of what you or I say." She paused. "They need us, they need you. You are their advocate. There is tea and coffee ready at the counter. I suspect the family won't be interested but please, help yourself."

Jordan nodded. It had been a long day for him, sometimes when the volunteers were called they didn't have time to eat or drink. He wandered over to pour himself a coffee. Jennifer returned to the little group.

"If you would like a tea or coffee, please, help yourselves," she said as Jordan sat down with his coffee.

"Jordan, can you introduce the family members to me?"

Jordan put his cup down. "This is Mr. and Mrs. Tompkins, and Devon's brothers Glenn and Thomas and his sister Marilee." Jennifer wrote down their names without looking down. Jordan picked up his coffee.

"Jordan mentioned you were looking for advice."

Again, no one answered. The same family member who she now knew as Glenn, who had glared at her at the front door continued to do so.

Jennifer waited for a few seconds. "My advice is simple. You will not remember the details of today, but you will remember today for the rest of your life. There is no rush to decide what to do, no major decisions need to be made immediately. You have options. Any questions?"

No questions were forthcoming.

"Do you have a minister or priest you would like to call?"

"No," responded Mr. Tompkins. "Don't put much stock in religion."

Silence. Jennifer pondered her next statement.

"What can you tell me about Devon?" she asked.

Glenn exploded. "He killed himself, that's what he did."

It was like a bomb dropped in the room. Jennifer braced herself for Glenn's next statements.

"He didn't have to do it. It's all Dad's fault."

The family all started talking at once, all except Mrs. Tompkins. Blame, fear, anger flew through the air. Jordan sat wide-eyed and silent.

Mr. Tompkins leapt to his feet and turned to Glenn.

"You ****, how dare you blame me for your brother's actions," he roared.

Jennifer chose to intervene rather than let the situation escalate. She stood.

"Mr. Tompkins," she said loudly, "Please, take a seat."

Mr. Tompkins was trembling with rage but he complied, turning his back to Glenn.

Jennifer stayed standing for a few seconds and looked at the family. Glenn was not ready to stop talking.

"Dad told my brother he was queer. Devon wouldn't hurt a flea. Dad called him names until he couldn't take anymore."

Jennifer cut into his tirade, hoping to find the words to get through to Glenn.

"Glenn," she said. "I am so sorry. Clearly you loved and understood your brother."

Again a cacophony of noise erupted, a family divided by a generation gap with different values.

Mr. Tompkins again tried to make himself heard. In his grief and rage he was having no part of accepting his deceased son's lifestyle.

"Shut up Sidney," said Mrs. Tompkins. "Just shut up for once." She started to cry. The family stopped talking, even Mr. Tompkins who was taken aback by his wife's command.

"Jennifer," continued Mrs. Tompkins. "I want my son to have a proper burial. We don't have much money."

Jennifer looked at the grieving mother. "That can be arranged. And if you need financial assistance and qualify, then help is available."

Mrs. Tompkins nodded.

Jennifer quickly outlined the resources available through social services, laid aside the form for them and added a few pamphlets.

She looked at the family. "Devon's life was important to everyone in this room. You can consider a celebration of his life without having a minister. Family, friends …"

At that point Glenn interrupted. "His partner."

Jennifer continued. "Devon's partner."

"I've had enough of this bull****", said Mr. Tompkins as he rose and left the room. No one followed. Jennifer heard the front door of the funeral home close.

"Mrs. Tompkins, I have the name of an agency that will help you and your husband with some his concerns around Devon's lifestyle. I will add it to this package I will be giving you."

Mrs. Tompkins nodded. "My husband is a stubborn man," she said. "But Devon was a good kid. He wouldn't hurt anyone." She started sobbing. "He didn't deserve this."

Jennifer's heart ached for Mrs. Tompkins. Her sons and daughter gathered around her, crying with her. At least Mrs. Tompkins didn't try to defend her husband, thought Jennifer. Mr. Tompkins was clearly being marginalized by his family. It would be a hard road ahead for him in his recovery from his son's death by suicide, that is, if he was able to recover.

Jordan rose to pour himself another coffee. Glenn followed, so did Marilee. The three of them stood at the counter talking quietly. Thomas sat beside his mother, holding her hand as she cried.

Jennifer gave them all the time they needed to talk. The funeral home line rang at one point during the hour the family started their grief work. Jennifer let the answering service pick it up, her phone was on vibrate. Mrs. Tompkins asked about burial and cremation, Jennifer gave her a few details. Marilee picked up one of the pamphlets on suicide and flipped through it, taking it over to Glenn when something caught her eye. Thomas did not leave his mother's side.

Finally, Mrs. Tompkins looked up at Jennifer. "Thank you," she said, her lip trembling. "Let's go," she said, turning to her family.

"I'll go find Dad," said Thomas as he headed out ahead of his siblings and mother. When they got to the door Thomas was re-entering. "No sign of him Mom."

"Then he will have to find his own way home," said Mrs. Tompkins firmly. She turned to Jennifer Their eyes met and Mrs. Tompkins hugged her for a long time then turned to let Jordan open the door for her. Glenn hugged Jennifer next, followed by Thomas and Marilee. Jordan looked at Jennifer.

"Thank you," he said.

"You're welcome Jordan," she said as she shut the door. She didn't expect to see the family again; it was possible they would go to another funeral home. At least I did my best to help, she thought. She glanced at her watch, saw that is was after 7 p.m., locked the door and shut down the funeral home. She checked her phone, Elaine had called earlier, she said it could wait.

Jennifer headed up the stairs to greet Grimsby, scooping him up and burying her head in his fur. He purred, his mistress was home and it was dinnertime. She just felt the comfort holding him gave her after dealing with the family's pain. She spent the rest of the evening in front of the TV, mindlessly watching a movie, Grimsby at her side.

The next day dawned with no word from the Tompkins' family. Jennifer thought of them often throughout the day and hoped they would be able to tap into some of the resources available to them.

Elaine called to ask Jennifer how things were and to ask if she preferred off-white or white. Jennifer laughed and told Elaine to pick whatever she liked. "I don't pretend to know anything about decorating," said Jennifer. "You are the expert."

"I'm no expert," laughed Elaine, "but I think the white looks better in the sunshine."

"Enjoy," said Jennifer. With Elaine off decorating, Jennifer was using her spare moments to work on her bookkeeping course. She didn't particularly like working with numbers, but found as she got into the course that bookkeeping simply meant keeping her ducks in a row and it suited her attention-to-detail personality. She explored other online learning options, determined to learn all she could about the business aspect of funeral service.

She was enjoying the quiet, there had been no calls for a few days. Gwen had popped over for a quick visit. Other than the occasional conversation with Drew and Elaine, it remained quiet.

Marcia and Phil arrived early the next afternoon for their evening in the Falls. As they entered the funeral home, Phil swept Jennifer up in a hug, twirling her around until they were both dizzy. Plunking her down he stood back and gave a low wolf whistle.

"Look at you, brat," he said, using one of his pet names for her. "All managerial and professional."

"Love your hair," Marcia enthused. "You look amazing. Phil's right, it gives you a certain level of maturity. Love the suit too."

"Thanks you two," said Jennifer, happy that her friends validated her new look. "Come on in—we have lots of catching up to do."

"Let's start with a tour," said Phil. "Marcia's told me a lot about this place. I like the location, the lot, and the access. Lots of room to maneuver."

"The flow of the rooms is well thought out," Marcia said to Phil. "Quick access to the chapel and the lounge is far enough away that the noise won't disturb the visitations."

"Reception is well-positioned too," said Phil as he and Marcia headed down the hall.

Jennifer held back and watched her friends with a smile. Phil and Marcia were in the second suite before they noticed her absence.

"Hey—get down here," said Phil as he poked his head around the door. No sooner were the words out of his mouth then the phone rang.

"I'll take over," said Marcia as Jennifer left to answer the phone. "Carry on."

It was another call. The family was phoning from out of town and would be arriving the next morning to make the arrangements. Jennifer discussed their options with them and agreed to call the hospital to see if the deceased had been released. How typical, she thought. Well laid plans interrupted. If she did the transfer before they went out for dinner then she would have all day tomorrow, hopefully, to prepare for the funeral. She called the hospital who confirmed the release.

She found Phil and Marcia in the lounge.

"Well?" said Marcia.

"A family is coming in tomorrow, just have to do the transfer. You guy's OK for about half an hour?"

"Where's Peter?" asked Marcia. "Can't he go?"

"Maybe. I'll see if he's free." A quick call to Peter took care of the transfer, he wished the three of them a merry evening.

"I feel guilty. Usually if I'm not busy I would take care of things like that."

"Well, get over it," said Marcia. "You are busy and your staff can handle it. The evening awaits."

Jennifer laughed. "Alrighty then, quick change and we are out of here. Come on up and say hi to Grimsby."

Grimsby was quite happy to meet Phil and see Marcia and they tossed his squeaky mouse around while Jennifer changed. She heard the garage door open and looking out of her bedroom window saw Peter's truck.

"All set," said Jennifer happily. "I'll take the Lincoln just in case I have to leave. I've been helping at Dimitri's funeral home for a few days. I was over there yesterday and called today, things are fine, so barring another call we have the evening ahead of us."

"I'll ride with the brat," said Phil. "You OK with

that Marcia?" He drew out the three syllables of Marcia's name into a long drawl.

"Yep. I'll see lots of the brat in the weeks and months ahead."

She made a face at Jennifer and the three of them left laughing.

The show and dinner and playtime meant their evening was filled with much needed laughter and merriment. Just after midnight, they sought out Gwen at her table, chatting briefly before Phil and Marcia left for Toronto.

Hugging each other tightly they said their goodbyes in the parking garage and went their separate directions. Jennifer felt lighter than she had over the past few weeks. I needed this time with my friends she thought, as she headed home. It was a perfect evening.

9

As Jennifer pulled the car into the funeral home lot, she parked the Lincoln near the garage door. She had her key ready and quickly unlocked the door, ensuring it was latched behind her. As she started upstairs she saw the bag of garbage she had planned on tossing in the dumpster earlier sitting near the door.

"Shoot," she said out loud. Putting her purse on the floor of the garage she picked up the garbage bag and using a nearby rain boot, propped open the door. She walked towards the dumpster, picking up a few pieces of paper along the way. Tossing the garbage in the large bin she turned and headed back to the funeral home. Spotting a paper cup lying nearby on the grass, she walked back, picked it up and tossed it out too. Glancing around to ensure there were no more loose bits of garbage, she headed back to the garage. A few feet from the door a ringtone, not hers, blasted. Someone cursed inside the garage.

Jennifer started to back up slowly. Fear gripped her, causing her to hold her breath. Her legs were like rubber. She reached into her pocket, pulled out her phone and with shaking hands, dialed 911.

"Police, fire or ambulance," on the second ring.

"Police, Spencer Funeral Home, intru—" She barely saw him coming. As he barreled into her the phone flew from her hand and skidded on the pavement. The fear, more intense than she had ever experienced, swept over her. She staggered from the body slam and felt herself being pulled inside the funeral home.

"No," she screamed.

"Shut up. Just shut up." The man dragged her inside, kicked the rain boot away and slammed the garage door, locking the latch behind them.

Travis, it must be Travis, she thought in her panic. She continued to struggle.

The intruder turned her around and slammed her again, this time into the van.

"Where is it?"

Looking up in the dark of the garage she saw his outline. It didn't sound like Travis.

"WHERE IS IT?" he yelled.

Jennifer realized that this person was a serious threat. From his brute strength she suspected he might be high on drugs. She had little chance at managing the intensity of his anger fueled by the drugs if that was the case. She had to stay calm. Her life could depend on it.

"What are you looking for?" her voice quivered.

"The money. What did you do with it?"

"I don't keep money in the funeral home," she said, knowing full well he would not believe her.

He grabbed her arm and shook her. "The money in the casket. Did you take it? You're dead if you did. It's mine."

Jennifer's fear kept her from thinking clearly. If she told him the police had it then he could kill her in his rage. If she played dumb she could stall for time in the hopes that the police would arrive. But the latch was on the garage door now, they wouldn't be able to break in. Think, Jennifer, think, she demanded.

"A casket?" she asked, doing her best to stay calm.

He yanked at her arm, half pulling and half dragging her down the hall to the selection room. He flicked on the lights, there were no windows in that room, the person knew they would not be seen from the outside.

He's been here before, thought Jennifer in the split-second it took her eyes to adjust to the light. She looked at his face.

"Jorge."

Anger, fierce and intense, swept over her. How dare he threaten her. How dare he use Uncle Bill's, no … *her* funeral home for illegal activity.

"Ya, me," said Jorge. "Now where is it?"

The anger took over; her fear minimized by the intensity of the new emotion.

"I'll give it to you, but I want answers."

Jorge looked at her. His pupils were pinpoints and she realized that he *was* on some kind of drug. Jorge had not thought things through or figured out that if she knew where the money was then it probably still wouldn't be there.

"You think you're so high and mighty owning a funeral home, better than the rest of us." He leaned into her, his breath putrid. "You're so stupid, Travis and me have a good thing going. You aren't going to ruin it."

Jennifer fought for composure. "What good thing?" Jorge's demise could be in his bravado and bragging—she intended to keep him talking.

"That casino boss, he thought he was high and mighty too. I took care of him. Tried to steal my money. He owed me." Jorge laughed derisively.

"So you killed him."

"Ya, I killed the SOB," said Jorge, leaning into her face again. "And I can kill you too. That casino dude, put the money in the casket. He was supposed to hand it to me. Then I had to go away on a job, he could have given it to me but he didn't."

Jennifer was having trouble matching the pieces

of Jorge's drug infused puzzle. Why would a casino boss bring money to a funeral home? How did Travis factor into this? Why did the pit boss owe Jorge money?

"Alright," said Jennifer. "You can get your money."

"That's more like it," He pushed her farther forward into the selection room.

"So it was you that broke in," said Jennifer struggling to keep the conversation going.

"Didn't break in, just came to get what was owed me. Now show me."

Encroaching sirens shattered the stillness.

"Hurry up!

Jennifer closed her eyes briefly and ran through the inventory in her head. Recognizing that in his substance abused stupor it had not occurred to Jorge that the money would no longer be in the casket, she quickly planned her next move.

"This one," she said nodding toward the mahogany in the centre.

"Damn," said Jorge, "Travis gave me the wrong casket number."

"No," lied Jennifer. "He gave you the wrong manufacturer. It's this one".

Jorge did not release the grip on her arm as he pulled her toward the mahogany unit. The front lid was open; the bottom lid was closed. Jorge used his left hand to tug on the casket lid.

It didn't budge. Grinding his teeth with rage he turned to Jennifer.

"Calm down, it's latched on the inside," said Jennifer, her strategy threatened by Jorge's frustration and anger.

Jorge reached under the lower lid, found the latch. He let go of Jennifer's arm and opened the lid. Jennifer stood at the foot of the casket, her heart pounding, waiting for an opportunity to make a move.

She had not counted on Jorge pulling a knife from his pocket. He flicked open the blade and slashed the velvet material and started digging through the cotton bedding.

"It's on the bottom in the middle," said Jennifer.

Stepping back once, and another to the side Jennifer threw all her energy into the heavy lid, slamming it hard on Jorge's neck and shoulders. Jorge screamed. She ran for the hallway to the garage. A man stood there, blocking her way.

"No!" she screamed. It was like hitting a wall. He tried to grab her shoulders.

"It's OK Jennifer. It's me, Travis."

Travis. In her blind panic she knew she had to get past him to safety. Kicking hard at his knee she managed to turn back, running through the selection room into the lounge. Out of the corner of her eye she could see Jorge, his face contorted with fury and pain. She opened the opposite door of the selection room into the lounge and ran through to the front office. For a split second she debated whether or not to hide under the big desk or flee out the front door. The shouting behind her made the decision easier, she would take her chances at the door.

As she yanked the door open she saw the flashing lights of a cruiser and the silhouette of a policeman.

10

Detective Sergeant Gillespie looked closely at Jennifer. They were sitting in the funeral home lounge, she was in shock and shivering. She learned later from Peter that when the police were unable to access the garage door, they thought they might have a hostage situation on their hands. They had found her phone on the pavement, looked up Peter's number, called him and rushed a squad car over for the keys to the front door.

"Jennifer put up a good fight for such a tiny person," he said to the female officer sitting slightly behind him, adding "Travis took a hit from her too."

An officer handed Jennifer a cup of tea, the same woman who attended the break-in days earlier. Jennifer had been wrapped in a blanket and was now silently rocking back and forth.

"Are you sure you don't want to go to hospital?" asked Detective Sergeant Gillespie.

She looked at him dully and shook her head as she accepted the tea. If she had followed his advice, she thought, the garbage would have sat there until morning. If Jorge had turned the knife on her in his drug-fueled rage, the outcome could have been fatal. If the police had not shown up … she squeezed her eyes shut. She took a few sips of the tea and put the cup down.

Reaching over, Detective Sergeant Gillespie took her hand and squeezed it gently. Jennifer barely noticed. He turned to the female officer sitting slightly behind him. "I'm worried about her. She's usually pretty feisty."

The female officer nodded and Jennifer heard her say she was glad the outcome had not been more serious.

Jennifer opened her eyes, glanced at the Detective Sergeant's hand over hers and, looking up, met his eyes. She saw compassion and concern written all over his face. She glanced over at the female officer who was also showing concern. The female officer smiled at Jennifer, then looked down at Detective Sergeant Gillespie's hand over hers, then looked back at Jennifer and winked.

The wink that made Jennifer realize her ordeal was really over. Pulling her hand away she sat up, picked up her cup, took another sip and confronted the Detective Sergeant.

"Where's Jorge?" Her voice was stronger this time, and she made it clear by her tone she expected an answer. She noticed his grin. He leaned back in his chair and crossed his legs.

"Jorge is in hospital."

Jennifer interrupted him. "Did Travis hurt him? I heard shouting."

"No, you did. Slamming the casket lid on him was a smart move. He has a fractured clavicle."

"Then where's Travis?"

Detective Sergeant Gillespie let out a small sigh and, turning to the officer, said, "Would you mind getting Mr. Holden?" The woman rose and left the room.

Jennifer stiffened. Why is Travis still here, she thought. "Shouldn't he be in jail by now?"

"Travis was working with us."

He entered the room, followed by the other officer. He was limping a bit.

Before anyone could get a word out, Jennifer turned to him, "How did you get in? What were you doing here and why was there money in the casket? Jorge told me you were involved. Why did you try to run us off the road?"

Travis didn't miss a beat, "I'm sorry Jennifer. I was following orders; the police were close to making some arrests."

"I'm listening," said Jennifer turning to Detective Sergeant Gillespie.

Between Detective Sergeant Gillespie and Travis, the story came out. Jennifer listened intently as the detective explained that the casino pit boss had a side business that involved drugs, money laundering, and other shady deals. He had been under observation for some time. He was usually careful about who he recruited to work for him. His fatal mistake was recruiting Jorge, a loose cannon with a big ego. Jorge had worked for the pit boss selling drugs for about three months. He was ruthless and loyal but starting to get greedy. He was also addicted to the products he sold. The pit boss was supposed to meet Jorge in the funeral home parking lot the day he died, to give him the money to buy drugs.

"Why here?" asked Jennifer. "Why not at another location?"

Detective Sergeant Gillespie continued, "Jorge was also under surveillance; he spotted one of the undercover officers near Williams Funeral Home and was spooked. Jorge drove the limo from time to time for Travis, I mean, Spencer Funeral Home, and figured it was a safe place to meet. It's quiet, not the sort of location that attracts attention, and it was convenient. Both Jorge and the pit boss would look like they had legitimate business at the funeral home.

"Jorge had been ordered to pick up a substantial shipment of drugs, the pit boss was supplying the cash. When the pit boss came to the parking lot to drop off the payment, Jorge was a no show; he had been sent on an out of town transfer. The pit boss called him; Jorge told him to put it in a safe place at the funeral home where he could retrieve it later, or he would pick it up at the pit boss's house the next morning. The pit boss told Jorge he would leave it at the funeral home.

"Why did the pit boss not take it back with him?" asked Jennifer.

"Because he didn't want to risk getting caught with such a large sum and he didn't want Jorge anywhere near his house," said Detective Sergeant Gillespie. "He was used to surveillance at the casino and was very cautious about carrying anything that could implement him in a crime. The pit boss always made sure he didn't miss any time at the casino, it was his alibi and cover for a lot of his dealings. So the pit boss entered the funeral home carrying a briefcase and pretended to be an executor."

"I believed him," said Travis. "He was a smooth talker and said he wanted to make a couple of prearrangements. We discussed pricing, I took him around the funeral home, showed him the suites. We were just entering the selection room when the phone rang. I excused myself and went to the front office to answer it. It was your lawyer calling to inform me that you were taking over the business the next day. The call was fairly brief."

Travis went on, "The pit boss took those two

minutes to look around and used the opportunity to put the cash in the casket while I was talking. I was just coming back from the office and saw him poking around the bottom of the casket, backed off for a bit and waited to enter the selection room. I made a note later of the casket make and number."

Detective Sergeant Gillespie picked up the story, "The pit boss thought he'd found a safe place to hide the money and Jorge could pick it up anytime. But he underestimated Jorge's loyalty. Jorge kept calling the pit boss at work that night. The pit boss chose not to call him back from the casino, he didn't want to risk getting caught on surveillance. An angry Jorge showed up at his house the next day. He threatened the pit boss, found out where the money was and pulled a gun."

Travis jumped in, "The pit boss called on the pretext of asking for the casket model and make for his 'prearrangement'. He described it perfectly. I gave him the make and model."

Detective Sergeant Gillespie continued, "Jorge's plan was to kill the pit boss and keep the money for himself. He forced him to drive to the field where he executed him. He then ditched the pit boss' car in a parking lot at the falls and took a bus back home. By then it was morning and there were too many people around to break in and find the casket with the cache inside.

"Travis had called the police right after the pit boss left the funeral home. The police met Travis offsite and connected him with the Ontario Provincial Police major crimes unit. The decision was made to have Travis call Jorge, let him know he'd seen the pit boss put the money in the casket, and tell Jorge he wanted a cut. The police would then catch Jorge with the money."

"Unfortunately," added Detective Sergeant Gillespie, "the major crimes unit did not communicate quickly enough with the local division. Jorge had the casket number and description from the pit boss. He was to meet Travis at the corner; the plan was to arrest him once he set foot on the property. Jorge had other ideas though. He wasn't going to wait for Travis. When you and your friend were heading out to dinner Jorge had just broken in, he was hiding in the dark in the selection room. When you left, he searched the casket. He had started to search all of them, something spooked him and he slipped out. He was sitting in his car across the street trying to call Travis when you and Marcia returned from the transfer."

"When you found the money in the casket, the officers who responded to the call knew nothing about the possible connection to the homicide or who may have been involved. From their perspective you had hidden it there, although it didn't make a lot of sense at the time. They still had a job to do, hence all the questions."

"The security team that reported the break-in to the division office threw us a bit too. Why was there a security team outside your funeral home? There were more than a few questions raised as a result of that call." Jennifer chose not to interrupt at that point to explain, the police did not need to know who her clients were. By law, the security firm would be required to identify themselves to police. It was taking all the mental energy she could muster to listen to what Travis and Detective Sergeant Gillespie were telling her.

Detective Sergeant Gillespie continued, "The end result was that we felt that the attempted sting to catch Jorge was a bust. We believed he knew the money was gone and we stopped surveillance."

"Then why did you come to the funeral home to warn me?" asked Jennifer.

Detective Sergeant Gillespie became pensive. "Right after the break in, we honestly thought he had given up and was smart enough to realize the money was gone. We didn't catch him in the act. But because I didn't believe you were involved, because I felt something wasn't quite right and I was annoyed that the major crimes unit had not communicated fully or co-operated with us at the local level, I just wanted to warn you to be careful."

His shoulders slumped and his head dropped. "I just wish we had been able to take the money from the casket ourselves as soon as we found out about it and bring Jorge in for questioning. It would have made all our lives easier." He looked up at Jennifer. "Especially yours."

The silence was poignant, each person in the room lost in thought. The female officer broke the silence. "I'm sorry Jennifer. When we showed up for the break-in and found the money, well ..."

"You were doing your job," said Jennifer.

"Yes, but it didn't make sense. The last thing we wanted to do was implicate you, you seemed genuinely upset by the break-in and you did call us; but when you pulled that money from the casket ..."

"A cache in a casket," said Jennifer. "The perfect hiding place."

No sooner were the words out of her mouth than her phone rang. It was Peter.

"Have to take this," said Jennifer to the two officers. She ignored Travis. She hit the answer button.

"Peter, thank you."

"Are you OK? The police were at my place. I promised you and Elaine I'd check on you, I feel awful."

"I'm fine Peter, honestly. And you can't be here twenty-four hours a day. I'll fill you in tomorrow.

It's late and we have a busy day coming up. The main thing is, it's over."

"You're sure?"

"Positive. I have your key, remind me tomorrow to give it back."

The relief in Peter's voice was clear. "I'm … I'm just glad nothing bad happened."

Jennifer reassured him again before disconnecting the call.

Peter's last statement bothered her; nothing bad happened? Something bad *had* happened. The police had suspected her of hiding the money; they had lied to her. She was bruised and stiff from her encounter with Jorge and Travis. She'd been traumatized twice in the past ten days with the break-ins. The visits from the police at night would give the neighbours plenty to gossip about. It could hurt the reputation of the funeral home, a reputation that was flawless when Uncle Bill was alive.

Suddenly Jennifer needed to be alone.

"Are we done?" she asked the two officers. Travis sat impassively.

Detective Sergeant Gillespie picked up on her tone. He studied her carefully. "You have every reason to be angry, and I suspect the next few days will be emotionally and mentally challenging for you.

We're done," he said as he and the other officer rose

to leave, Travis behind them. Jennifer didn't even get up to walk them out; she heard them exit through the front door. As soon as the door closed she rose, turned off the coffee and then checked to ensure both doors were locked tightly. Her mind had stopped processing. She didn't bother to turn off the lights to the lounge, just headed straight to her apartment and sat down on her couch. She hurt all over.

Grimsby met her at the door. Jennifer walked past him, sat on the couch and closed her eyes. Some part of her didn't see her pet; she didn't scratch behind him behind his ears, or cuddle him, or pet him or offer him a treat. She barely noticed when he jumped onto the coach and lay down beside her. A minute later she felt his paw on her arm, yet still kept staring into space. She didn't move until much later when her head slipped slightly sideways as she fell asleep.

11

Jennifer was lost. She wandered through a building with many rooms looking for Anne. When she tried to return to the last place they had been together, she seemed to be getting farther away from that spot. For what seemed like hours she wandered aimlessly through the building, getting nowhere.

A distant ringing caught her attention and it got louder, penetrating her consciousness, demanding her attention. Snapping awake she realized she was in her apartment, not in an obscure building looking for her sister. The ringing persisted and she reached for the phone—her mind on autopilot.

It was the answering service; the family who was to come in at 10 a.m. wanted to move the appointment up an hour, to 9 a.m. As Jennifer leaned over to pick up the pen and paper beside the phone, pain shot through her neck and shoulders. Scribbling down the number, she felt stiffness radiating in her hands. She hurt. She slowly got to her feet. Grimsby raised his head as his mistress got up; he stretched and yawned, jumping off the couch to head for his dish.

Jennifer glanced at the time. It was 8:35 a.m. She called the family, doing her best to keep the fatigue that threatened to drag her under out of her voice, and arranged to meet them at 9:15. She would have to process what had taken place after the family was taken care of. Grimsby was first though. She tossed him a treat, gave him fresh food and water and quickly scooped the litter.

She headed to the bathroom. Her suit was wrinkled, her hair a mess and she had dark circles under her eyes. She took a quick shower, longing to stay in the warmth, then put the blue suit on a chair to press later. She changed into her funeral suit. At 8:56 a.m. she headed downstairs to unlock the door and start the coffee. The funeral home was open and ready for the day. Jennifer wanted to be emotionally and mentally ready after last night's events but she had no interest. She was numb. She heard Peter come in. Heading to the lounge she saw him starting to dust the furniture. He was cleaning up the lounge from the night before.

He turned to her, his face portraying his concern. "Jennifer," he started.

"I'm fine Peter," she said with a smile she didn't feel. "Well, almost fine. A little sore."

He poured her a coffee.

"Have a family coming in a minute or so. I'll leave you to hold the fort and then we can catch up on last night's events. I could use some help strategizing." She pulled his key from her pocket and handed it to him.

Peter nodded. "Elaine will be here shortly too." Before she could respond, he added, "She said the cottage is nearly done. Just a few little finishing touches. She thought you might need a little down time, so she's coming in to help out."

The front door chimed.

"I'll get it," said Peter. "You haven't even had a sip of coffee." He headed to the front.

Jennifer took a deep breath. Having Peter and Elaine there made the day ahead much easier. She decided to let them in on the details and ask for their advice. She took a few sips of her coffee, put down the cup and went to the front office. Peter was settling the family in; he quietly withdrew and Jennifer sat down with her clients, immersing herself in their needs. An hour later they left to deal with the influx of family and friends and details that come with death. She reassured the family that when they returned to the funeral home, everything they had requested would be taken care of.

Elaine and Peter were talking quietly in the lounge when she entered. Elaine wordlessly came to her and hugged her gently, tears running down her face.

"Elaine, don't cry. Please don't. It's OK. We'll get through this, all of us." Jennifer found herself wiping her eyes too. Elaine's heartfelt hug and Peter's thoughtfulness at coming in early touched deeply.

"Peter, can you run out for the permits?" she asked. "When you get back, I'd like to have a staff meeting, but first I need to make a few calls. Elaine—the contract details for the call are on the front desk."

Elaine smiled as she wiped her eyes. "Right on it," she responded. "Come on Peter, let's get this day started."

As the two left the room Jennifer walked over, poured herself another coffee, and entered her little office, closing the door behind her. A few quick calls to the minister and cemetery took precedence. Once that had been completed, she took a deep breath and dialed her lawyer's office. The secretary answered on the second ring.

"It's Jennifer Spencer. Is Mr. Duncan in? There was an incident at the funeral home last night that requires his expertise and I would like to talk to him before the media contacts me."

"Just a minute Jennifer. I will check with him."

It was less than a minute before Mr. Duncan picked up the phone. "Hello Jennifer. How can I help?"

Jennifer outlined the recent events, starting with the break-in and moving into the previous evening. Mr. Duncan occasionally interrupted with questions and explained to Jennifer that she would probably have to go to court and that the media interest would likely be local only and would be able to get a copy of the police report.

"Think of yourself as the 'colour' for their story," said Mr. Duncan. "Once the reporter has all the details from the police report they will want the human side. Expect a call." He added, "Today's news is tomorrow's garbage. It will be over soon."

"Should I meet with them or just let them ask their questions over the phone?" Jennifer asked.

"They might want a picture of the caskets or the funeral home. It's the human interest side of a police matter they want."

"Colour," said Jennifer wryly. "I have lots of that: I am green and purple and yellow with bruises."

Mr. Duncan chuckled. "You'll be fine, I have every confidence in you. Call me if you have any more questions."

"Thanks Mr. Duncan. You've helped get things into perspective."

Her next call was to Anne. She expected to leave a voicemail but her sister picked up. After hearing Jennifer's story, Anne, for once, didn't fire a barrage of questions at her. She reiterated the media's role and gave her a few talking points. She then dropped a surprise of her own into the conversation.

"I have five days off and will be down in a couple of days. Are you up for it?"

Jennifer was thrilled. She and Anne did not get together very often. Things were looking brighter. The twins finalized the details of Anne's arrival and as Jennifer hung up, Elaine tapped on the door.

Jennifer rose, opened the door and walked into the lounge.

"A young man by the name of David called, he's with the local news. He'd like you to call him," said Elaine.

"I've been expecting that. Is Peter back?"

"Just got in," said Elaine.

"OK, I'll call the reporter ..." continued Jennifer as she looked at the slip of paper Elaine had passed to her. It took a few seconds for his name to register. "David." She glanced up at Elaine. "I'll be out in a few minutes."

A quick call to David reaffirmed everything Duncan and Anne had told her. He did want to come and take a picture of the funeral home rather than use a stock photo of a casket. He agreed to stop by in about an hour and a half.

Sitting down with her staff in the lounge,

Jennifer did her best to steer the discussion to make it about them too, how they felt, what they thought about the situation, how they believed it could affect the business. For over an hour the three of them discussed their fear of it happening again, of someone getting hurt, of what it could do to the reputation of the funeral home.

Jennifer explained that she had called her lawyer; she knew she would have to go to court to testify eventually and shared how she felt about that, and that if she needed help with public relations issues that help was available. She also said that Spencer Funeral Home and its staff were reputable and respected, and it was because of Elaine, Peter's and her efforts and Uncle Bill's legacy. She repeated the lawyer's statement about "tomorrows garbage". The three of them made a pact to keep an upbeat and positive attitude about what had taken place. Unspoken between them was the bond they shared and their commitment to the families they served. That always came first.

Right on time David, the reporter, showed up. He was no taller than Jennifer and he looked younger. Jennifer chuckled inwardly, he didn't look nearly as scary as she had made him out to be.

Leading him to the lounge, they sat. Jennifer offered him coffee or tea which he declined. She took the lead in the conversation.

"I'm sure you have a lot of work to do, and deadlines to meet," she said pleasantly. "How can I help?"

David pulled out a tape recorder and explained that he would like to record the conversation.

"Of course."

"How are you feeling after such an eventful night?"

"Bruised, sore, and tired, by the way. I'm sure you saw the police report."

"Yes. The intruder was looking for money?"

"A cache," responded Jennifer. David looked puzzled and referred to his notes. "In a casket," prompted Jennifer.

"A casket cache. Good headline. Did you know the intruder?"

"Not really. He was a contract worker for another firm. He had apparently been here a few times before I took over the business and only once since I came."

"The police report states he was taken to hospital. How was he injured?"

"I slammed the lid of the casket on him. He had a knife and he was a threat."

David's eyebrows rose. "You sent him to hospital?"

"It was him or me."

"How did the money get in the casket?"

"Good question. You'd have to check the police report; I have no idea."

Not a bad deflection, thought Jennifer to herself. Anne would be proud. Truth was, she didn't believe the whole story.

David spent the next few minutes on background information such as when she moved to the Niagara region, how long she had been in the funeral home, etc. Eventually he stood up.

"Would it be possible to get a picture of a casket?" he asked politely.

"Certainly," said Jennifer matching his tone. "This way." She led him to the door off the lounge that entered the casket room. As she put her hand on the door knob she turned to him.

"Have you been in a room full of caskets before?"

"Uh ... no."

"Then I should fill you in before we enter. You will see about twelve caskets of various materials, wood, metal or cloth covered. There will be urns on shelves around the room. If you are uncomfortable we could set up a single casket outside the room for you."

"Umm, well, no; it should be OK," he said. Jennifer could tell he was trying to be professional, a position she had found herself in many times. She had not always been successful and it made her think of her first few contacts with Detective Sergeant Gillespie. She felt considerable empathy for the poor kid.

David was a trooper. He initially paled a bit upon entering, but Jennifer kept up a pleasant banter about the types of caskets and he rallied quickly. He took a couple of pictures of the caskets, checked them, then pronounced the photo-op successful.

She walked David to the door, where they shook hands. Coming up the walk was Detective Sergeant Gillespie.

"Thank you David," she called after him as she stood back to let the Detective Sergeant in.

"Isn't that the reporter from the regional paper?" asked Detective Sergeant Gillespie.

"It is. Come on in, let's sit in the lounge."

She poured a coffee for the Detective Sergeant and sat down. She assumed correctly that he was there to let her know what to expect next—what could happen in court.

Jennifer thanked him for his support and the support of his team last night. She told him that if there were any residual emotional effects from the incident that she would get help. Detective Sergeant Gillespie admitted that he too needed outside support once in a while, which surprised Jennifer a little. Not all front-line workers saw themselves as vulnerable, even though every one of them were.

"I do have a question for you. Why was Travis in the back hall at the prep room? And why was Travis so readily available?"

Detective Sergeant Gillespie's response was brief. "He insisted."

Jennifer cocked her head. "Why?"

"He's been staying in town here between assignments. We called him right away, we weren't sure where you or Jorge were in the funeral home. He knew his way through the funeral home. He was supposed to sneak back and open the garage door. We didn't have a lot of time; we knew Jorge was a loose cannon."

Jennifer felt uneasy with that statement. She wasn't sure she could or ever would trust Travis. If he was supposed to open the garage door, then what was he doing in the prep room hallway? Did he overhear them in the selection room and think he could stop Jorge? She did feel somewhat comfortable with the thought that Jorge or Travis would not be back.

As Detective Sergeant Gillespie rose to leave he pointed out the bruising on her wrist.

"You put up quite a fight last night. You must be pretty sore."

Jennifer laughed, "You should see the other guy. But yes, I am a little the worse for wear."

Detective Sergeant Gillespie smiled his crooked grin, "Jorge needed major surgery on his shoulder. He'll be out of hospital and in jail in the next day or so. Hopefully he won't be able to post a bond with his pending charge of first degree murder, plus his charges of break and enter. We'll let you know."

"Thanks," she responded as she walked him to the door.

Jennifer let Peter and Elaine know she'd be in the prep room and went to work.

By late afternoon everything was ready for the evening visitation. Jennifer went upstairs, had a quick snack and a bit of playtime with Grimsby. Downstairs she told Peter and Elaine that Anne was coming for a visit. The two of them exchanged glances and smiled.

"She's not the only one," said Peter. Marcia stepped around the corner.

"Marcia? Oh my gosh! What are you doing here?" The two friends hugged and cried while Peter and Elaine looked on, smug and happy co-conspirators in the surprise.

"Elaine called me last night. I am officially finished work," explained Marcia. I had vacation time coming, my replacement was able to start early, so I came down to look for condos. My furniture is going to storage.

"The cottage is ready," said Elaine. "My husband is finishing the rest today. I can't wait to show you Marcia."

"Can't wait to see it. Jennifer told me what you were doing—sounds beautiful."

Jennifer was at a loss for words. She looked at the three of them standing in front of her.

"Oh, one more thing," said Peter. "I almost forgot. He reached into his inside pocket and pulled out an envelope. "Anne asked me to give this to you and told me to tell you to pack your bags."

"I can't go anywhere," said Jennifer as she opened the envelope. "I haven't even been on the job a month yet." She scanned the page and sank into the nearest chair. Anne had booked them a four day trip to Vegas. It was Anne's way of winding down from the stress of her job, she loved Vegas, they both did.

"I hope you don't mind if I stay here until you get back from your trip," said Marcia, her smile lighting up her face.

"Of course not. Grimsby will be delighted." She scanned the ticket, taking in the details. "I am leaving after the funeral tomorrow?"

"Yep, you fly out at 10:30 p.m. which means you have to leave for the airport before 5 p.m." laughed Peter. "No sleep for you. I'll drive you to the airport. Anne will meet you there."

"Why don't you and Marcia head upstairs and

catch up? Elaine and I can cover visitation, you can greet the family and then relax for the rest of the evening."

Jennifer rose. "Thank you guys. I can't believe you managed all this. I have no words …"

"Off you go," said Elaine happily. "And you are very welcome."

Grimsby was at the door ready to greet his favourite visitor. Marcia scooped him up, sank onto the couch and cuddled him.

Jennifer poked her head in the fridge. "Salad and hamburger OK? Or would you prefer spaghetti?"

"Salad and a burger sound perfect," said Marcia. Jennifer pulled out the ingredients and got to work. "What are you going to wear in Vegas?" asked Marcia.

"I'll take one nice outfit but for the most part, jeans and t-shirts. We do a lot of walking and exploring when we aren't playing. I want to take Anne to the Titanic exhibit. I went a few years ago; it's quite remarkable."

Over dinner the two discussed Marcia's upcoming move and how they would arrange a call schedule and divide the workload. Jennifer was keen on getting Marcia up to speed on the business side and Marcia was amenable to learning.

Marcia cleaned up while Jennifer started

packing. She didn't quite fill her carry on; she was a light packer and planned to top it up with t-shirts and souvenirs for the staff. She was starting to feel excited about the trip.

A few minutes before 7 p.m., Jennifer went downstairs, greeted the family, asked if they had any questions about the funeral the next day and then, once they were settled, went back up to visit with Marcia. She came down again close to 9 p.m. to say goodnight to everyone. Peter and Elaine cleaned and locked up for the night.

Jennifer headed to bed shortly after she went upstairs for the final time. She hurt all over and was emotionally drained. She climbed into bed without Grimsby, who had attached himself to Marcia—watching TV. She fell quickly into a dreamless sleep.

Jennifer woke early the next morning. Heading out to the kitchen she made coffee and stood at the window by the deck. The sky was clear; it would be a good day for the funeral. She sat quietly at her kitchen table for a while reflecting on the events of the past few days. Glancing at the clock she rose, got ready, and checked her phone. Anne had texted her from the airport in Ottawa, she was getting ready to take an early flight. She had decided to meet her at the departure entrance and told Jennifer to text her when she and Peter were close.

Jennifer headed downstairs a few minutes before 8:30 a.m. Marcia was stirring as she left the apartment. As Jennifer turned the lights on she heard Peter come in, followed shortly by Elaine. Marcia joined them by 9:15 a.m.

"Jorge won't be driving the limo today," said Jennifer, a slight tinge of sarcasm in her voice. "I'll get you to keep an eye on the new driver Peter."

"Sure thing," said Peter. "The new guy will get briefed when he arrives."

As visitors started arriving and the phone started ringing, each person went to work. Marcia was in the front hall and Jennifer had just entered the front office to order the business cards with Marcia's name on them when the door opened. Marcia turned to greet the visitor.

"Is Ms. Spencer in?" said a familiar voice. It was the Detective Sergeant.

Jennifer turned around and walked toward him. "Marcia, this is Detective Sergeant Gillespie. Marcia has joined us full time. She's a funeral director from Toronto."

He shook her hand. "Nice to meet you Marcia, have you settled in yet?" he asked warmly.

"Looking for a condo in the Falls at this point," responded Marcia.

"Oh," said Detective Sergeant Gillespie. "I have a sister in the business, she might be able to help. In fact, I know of one unit that is about to go up for sale. It's good a value, a two bedroom."

"That would be great," responded Marcia.

He pulled his card and handed it to her. "Call me later, I'll speak to her and we can get started."

Jennifer watched the ease of their interaction with interest. Marcia was a tall and attractive young woman and Jennifer could tell she instantly made an impression on the Detective. Her lip twitched at the "we can get started" part. The usually reticent Detective Sergeant was showing a subliminal spark of interest in her friend.

"Jennifer, could we have a quick moment to talk. In fact, if the rest of the staff is free, can they join us?"

"Sure. I'll round up Peter and Elaine and meet you in the lounge."

Marcia and Detective Sergeant Gillespie were chatting condos when the rest of the team joined them.

"I'll get right to it," said Detective Sergeant Gillespie. "Jorge escaped from the hospital last night."

Somehow the news came as little surprise to Jennifer, although she did hear Elaine's sharp intake of breath. Peter scowled.

"He's in a sling, he can't use his arm so we don't think he can get too far. Apparently he was a little out of control post op; he is very angry with the police and with you Jennifer. We'd like to post an officer in the funeral home during business hours and put someone outside as well until he is apprehended."

"Did he direct any of his anger toward Travis?" asked Jennifer.

Detective Sergeant looked surprised. "No, I don't think so."

"Doesn't that seem a little odd?" asked Jennifer. "Where is Travis now?"

"I don't know." He looked at Jennifer pensively but did not add anything more to the conversation.

"Jennifer will be away for a few days," said Peter. "You should have Jorge in custody by the time she returns, correct?" There was a touch of disgust in his voice. Jennifer jumped in before Detective Sergeant Gillespie could answer.

"I'm concerned about all of you. Please let the police do their job and don't go anywhere without teaming up."

"There is an officer on the way over. He should be here in a few minutes. He is plainclothes, we don't wish to interrupt your business."

"Fair enough," said Jennifer. She looked around at her staff. "Any questions?"

No one answered, they just shook their heads no. Jennifer rose. "Thanks for the heads up. Let's just pray this has a good outcome," she said to Detective Sergeant Gillespie.

Marcia walked the Detective Sergeant out, the two of them continuing their earlier condo conversation. A man in a suit came up the path. He nodded briefly to the Detective but didn't speak. Entering the funeral home, he looked around, pulled a badge and told the staff he'd like to familiarize himself with the funeral home layout. Peter stepped up and gave him a tour. He asked to see the apartment and Jennifer reluctantly took him upstairs.

Grimsby wasn't upset by the visitor, which made Jennifer feel better. Grimsby was her radar and if he didn't like someone, then Jennifer took that seriously. The officer checked the patio doors and security bars, looked at the locks on the windows and reminded Jennifer to make sure she was locked in at night.

"You may want to tell Marcia as well," said Jennifer. "I'll be leaving for a few days. She'll be here alone. She wasn't part of this fiasco, she just arrived yesterday."

"I will. Don't worry, this isn't my first rodeo. If you all have cell phones, I'd like to be able to text you."

Jennifer smiled in spite of herself at the "first rodeo" comment. He returned her smile and she took him downstairs. She knew Elaine would make sure he was comfortable, and he and his partner were fed. They gave him their cell phone numbers and went back to work.

When the family arrived the officer was nowhere to be seen, respectfully keeping his distance. During visitation he kept a low profile, watching the front door during the service, watching the visitors, blending in. Jennifer went into the office during the service.

"I'm glad you won't be here alone while we are at the cemetery," said Jennifer.

"Me too," said Elaine. "This situation seems to have no end in sight."

Much to Peter's delight Drew, the new apprentice at Williams Funeral Home, was driving the limo. Jennifer watched the two of them interact and was pleased to see them get along so well. Jennifer focused on the task at hand. She had learned to block out external distractions when she was working and she put Jorge out of her mind. Even driving the procession didn't cause her as much anxiety as she was used to.

After the funeral they all pitched in to clean up. In the lounge Peter spoke up.

"Let's go boss, you have a plane to catch."

"But it's only 4 p.m." Secretly she was eager to go, even if it was a bit early.

"I put your suitcase in the trunk of the lead car right after the funeral," said Marcia. "Go change, and leave us alone."

Everyone laughed as she left for her apartment. It felt good to put on her jeans and sneakers. Back downstairs Marcia and Elaine did a checklist.

"Passport?"

"Credit card?"

"Ticket?"

"Phone?"

"Yes, yes and yes," said Jennifer. "I left some money on the table for groceries and cat food, Marcia."

"Then get out!" yelled Marcia. And with that Jennifer and Peter left the funeral home, laughter following them. The officer in the funeral home and outside in the van watched diligently as they pulled away.

12

The trip to the airport passed quickly. Peter talked about his family and hinted that he was considering making a change. Jennifer questioned him but he wasn't forthcoming, just stating that he was looking into something and would let her know when he had something concrete to tell her. She texted Gwen to say goodbye and then sat back to watch the city get closer. Finally, she broached the subject on her mind.

"Peter, I can't shake the feeling that somehow this isn't over."

He was pensive and pondered his reply carefully, "You're not given to a lot of drama Jennifer. So what is it you're concerned about?"

"Travis. He just seemed to be in the right places at the right time. Example—why was he speeding away from Niagara Falls after the pit boss was murdered? Why is he hanging around the Niagara region? He could be working anywhere in the province." Her shoulders slumped. "I don't know, I just don't know," she said, defeat reflected in her voice.

Peter chose to change the subject. "Almost there," he said, his tone upbeat.

Jennifer looked up at the airport signs and texted Anne to let her know they were pulling up. "Perhaps I am over thinking it. Maybe the trauma of the past few days and the learning curve involved in taking over the funeral home has clouded my thinking."

Peter flicked the blinker on for the airport lanes. "Hopefully once Jorge is back in custody things will settle down," he said kindly. "I for one will be happy to see him off the streets. We all will."

"Let me know the second you find out the police have him, will you? I need to know, whatever the hour."

"You know I will. You most of all need to hear he's in custody." He steered toward the Departure lanes. "I don't know what the appeal of Vegas is," laughed Peter, changing the subject again. "Give me a trip to Algonquin Park, a canoe and a tent any day."

"And bugs and bears and moose," Jennifer sung, responding to the mood change. "Oh—there's Anne!" She was almost bouncing with excitement. Her stomach was all butterflies. The second the car stopped she headed to her twin and threw her arms around her, squealing with joy. Anne responded with more reticence but was obviously pleased to see her too.

Peter unloaded the bag, waving goodbye as he pulled away and the two headed into the terminal, Jennifer chattering non-stop and Anne listening. Jennifer loved the airport, for her one of the best parts of travelling was the journey. She tried to take it all in, doing her best to set aside the heaviness of her mood that had consumed her the past few days. With a few hours to spare, she and Anne sought out a restaurant where they could watch planes take off and land, enjoy dinner and a drink, and talk about the cottage, their work and Vegas. They continued to catch up through security and customs and check in. But only once they were airborne did Jennifer broach the story of the cash in the casket.

"Once we land in Vegas," she said. "Don't let me talk about this OK? We're on vacation."

"Better not. I need this break. So do you. I get enough of this at work."

Anne supported Jennifer's idea that there was more to the story. She didn't diminish her sister's feelings. As the flight approached McCarran in Vegas, Jennifer and Anne were glued to the window as the plane banked. With the lights of the strip in view the two of them felt like kids going to Disneyworld.

As the plane landed so did Jennifer's heaviness of mood. She could hardly wait to disembark and take the monorail through the airport to the shuttle bus. She and Anne didn't mind waiting for the shuttle, they didn't mind the line up for registration once they got to their hotel; they had four days ahead of them.

Dumping their bags in their room they headed straight for a restaurant, getting sidetracked more than once on the way. They had a late dinner and re-energized before playing slots for a few hours then going to bed.

Jennifer didn't see the texts until the next morning when she checked her phone.

One was from Elaine. Jorge had been found and was back in hospital. She didn't elaborate, she just told Jennifer and Anne to have fun. Marcia texted to say that she was working with Chaplain Clive Griffith who had called just after Jennifer left. She also said that she was going to look at a condo later that day. She and Peter had done a coroner's call and everything was going well. She signed off with, *no more texts—have a great time.* Peter's text was brief: *they got him.*

Jennifer chose to heed her friend's advice. With Jorge back in custody, she put thoughts of the funeral home out of her mind. Vegas was calling.

"Let's do the Titanic exhibit today," said Anne over breakfast. "When that's done we can explore, maybe have dinner at one of the buffets."

"Sure," said Jennifer cheerfully. She had no agenda, no need to be somewhere or do something.

The Titanic exhibit held their interest for the rest of the morning. When they were handed their ticket they were told that they had the name of one of the real passengers on their ticket and at the memorial wall as they exited they would find out if they lived or died. For over three hours they immersed themselves in history, moving from the steerage to first class, reading every detail. The personal belongings of the passengers; the class differences sobered them. At the grand staircase they had their photo taken. As they wound their way to the end of the exhibit Jennifer found out that her passenger died, Anne's had survived. Both girls had visited the Titanic graveyard in Halifax. Standing at the list of the passengers names Anne turned to her twin.

"Kind of sobering isn't it?"

Jennifer just nodded. They spent part of the afternoon wandering through several hotels before they settled in at one of the casinos to play for a bit before dinner. The drink person was attentive and having downed several Caesars they got the giggles.

"I haven't this been tipsy in a long time," said Anne happily. No sooner were the words out of her mouth when her machine hit a bonus. The two of them watched as the machine ran through the free spins. In the blink of an eye, Anne hit it big.

"Wow," said Anne breathlessly, looking at the *call attendant* notice showing $930. "Wow. This just paid for my trip."

Jennifer was jumping up and down in her chair with excitement, clapping her hands like a little kid.

"Oh my gosh Anne, that's awesome! See, no good deed goes unpunished, you paid for my trip and look what happened," she said.

Anne looked over at her twin. "Methinks you have that saying out of context," she said.

"Doesn't matter. I'm really happy for you. A jackpot! You deserve it."

"I do," said Anne, putting on pretentious airs. "I do."

"You're lucky that's under the limit for the IRS," said Jennifer. "Gwen was telling me she had a $1200 win on one of her trips down and it took over 18 months to get the balance. Mind you, any win is a good one."

"Exactly. Which is why I'm heading straight back to the hotel and putting this in the safe."

Once the slot attendant had paid them and Anne had tipped her, the two of them walked back to the monorail and stopping long enough for Jennifer to pick up a few t-shirts at one of the Vegas shops. Back at the hotel Anne put her winnings in the safe and flopped on the bed.

"Now what?" she asked.

"How about a show tonight? Do you want to see if we can get tickets to a musical?"

"Sure." Anne closing her eyes. "I'm easy."

Jennifer called the concierge and, after a long discussion, hung up.

"Success. We have tickets to Menopause, the Musical."

Anne's eyes popped open. "What?? You're joking, right?"

"No. I know it's a bit before we're ready for that stage of life but it's got good reviews and it's supposed to be funny."

Anne rolled her eyes. "I beg to differ, it's more than a bit, it's decades."

Jennifer took the time to dress up a bit. Anne, for all her grumbling, did the same. They hopped the monorail and had dinner at the hotel.

The show turned out to be hysterical, the two of them laughing until it hurt. Afterwards, they stopped at a little bar, sat and had a drink.

"I could get used to this," said Anne contentedly.

"I could too, for a while. But this isn't the real world, and we're not the type of people to indulge constantly."

"True that," mused Anne. "But it's fun while it lasts."

The next few days flew by. They visited the Bellagio

fountain and conservatory and tearoom, went up the Eiffel tower and explored Freemont street. They walked in and out of hotels and casinos, stopping to play and browse and people watch. On their last morning Jennifer, who loved to play blackjack on one of her computer games, suggested they try a table.

"You go ahead, I'll watch," said Anne.

"That's no fun. I can coach you."

"Naw. I'll watch."

Gwen had coached Jennifer well. When Gwen played, she went at least twenty hands. It took a while for a five dollar table to open up, but one eventually did and Jennifer slipped into the seat.

"A hundred dollars please," she said to the dealer who counted out her twenty chips.

"That's a bit steep," said Anne dryly.

"It is, but Gwen does well and she taught me well. It's worth a try and life's all about trying."

"You ladies from Canada?" asked the dealer.

"We are," said Jennifer with a smile. "What gave us away?"

"Your accents," said the dealer. "*Aboot.*"

"Honestly, we do not say 'aboot', it's about," said Anne with mock indignity.

"And you're twins, double trouble," added the dealer. "Lord have mercy."

Every time Jennifer won a hand she put both

chips to the right. She and the dealer kept up a running banter, much to the amusement of the two other players at the table. She doubled down successfully on a split and set all four chips aside. When her chips on the left were gone she asked the dealer to cash her out, setting aside a chip for his tip.

"Quitting so soon?" asked the dealer.

"Don't chase my losses. And I prefer to quit while I'm ahead." She was thirty-five dollars over her hundred. "That pays one night tourist tax, and I still have my hundred," she said to Anne as the two of them walked over to the cashier's cage.

She checked her watch. "Guess we should pack up and get ready for the airport, the shuttle leaves in a little over an hour. I have just enough time to stop at the Vegas store and get the rest of the souvenirs."

On the way to the airport the two of them looked at the all the photos on their phone. There was a great selfie of them outside Paris at the foot of the Eiffel tower. "I think I'll text Peter, Elaine and Marcia and send this picture with a 'see you soon' message," said Jennifer. She sent the text and settled back in her seat with a sigh.

"Another memorable vacation. Let's do it again next year."

"Let's," said Anne. "Only next time, see if we can save enough for seven days."

All too soon they had cleared security and were

at the boarding gate. They watched the crew getting ready and looked at their fellow passengers, many of whom were dozing.

Anne fell asleep shortly after takeoff. Jennifer, who had the window seat, looked down at the clouds. She kept her eyes glued to the window hoping to see the Grand Canyon and the Laramie mountains, which on a good day were a beautiful pink. She was rewarded with a glimpse of them as they sparkled pink and coral in the sun. With a sigh of pleasure, she sat back in her seat and pulled out her phone, hitting her Kindle app. She read for about an hour, then put her phone away. Anne was still asleep beside her.

Wish I could sleep on a plane, she thought. Anne's so lucky. Jennifer let her thoughts wander back to Niagara and her funeral home. The trauma of the past weeks seemed minor now. She thought back to Jorge's chatter in the selection room: how the pit boss owed him, how Travis and he were buddies, how Travis had given him the wrong casket number. Why did it keep coming back to Travis?

Then it hit her with a force almost as real as a punch. Jorge said Travis gave him the casket number. Detective Sergeant Gillespie said the pit boss did. Why didn't I figure that out sooner, she said to herself. She pulled her phone and checked the time. They had another two hours before landing. I have to let Detective Sergeant Gillespie know, she thought.

Anne woke from her sleep about an hour out of Toronto. She wasn't chatty and Jennifer decided to keep the information to herself.

Upon landing they collected their bags and said goodbye, Anne heading off to take the commuter flight to Ottawa. They hugged for a long minute, happy to have had the time together. Jennifer watched her sister walk towards the domestic flight area and felt herself choke up. When together they didn't always get along, but apart it was harder; she missed her twin, the one person who truly understood her.

She texted Peter to let him know he could enter the arrivals area and, dragging her suitcase, she headed toward the doors. He pulled up as she exited into the cool air. She was glad to be home.

"How was the trip?" Peter asked as he put her suitcase in the trunk.

"Fabulous, fun, magical, exciting—an adult Disneyland with amazing food and shows and exhibits," said Jennifer happily. How are things with you?"

"Amber is getting over her morning sickness, thank goodness, and the munchkin is tearing up the house. The funeral home was busy when you were gone: we had a coroner's call, Marcia did a call with a chaplain, and there were two funerals and a cremation.

"Wow. It was so quiet last week."

"Feels like I just dropped you at the airport yesterday," laughed Peter. "So did you win?"

"Anne hit a jackpot, I came home with a bit more than I took," replied Jennifer.

"Really? What's your secret?"

"No secret, I count my spins. If I put in twenty dollars at fifty cents a spin I do forty spins and cash out. That's my winnings and I try not to play that money. If I hit over ten dollars early, I cash out again. Made a little bit on blackjack. Course, sometimes I just keep going, then I usually lose."

She pulled her phone out and texted Gwen. *I'm baack.* Gwen came back immediately with a smiley face and, *can't wait to hear about it!*

Settling back in her seat Jennifer broached the subject most on her mind.

"Tell me about Jorge."

Peter glanced over at her. He hesitated before answering.

"Jorge was a victim of a hit and run."

"Hit and run or attempted homicide?" asked Jennifer. Peter looked surprised. "I looked back at the texts from you guys you sent my first day away. They were a bit cryptic and I put two and two together."

"The police aren't saying anything. A motorist found him lying by the side of the road at the edge of town. The last I heard, which was a couple of days ago, Marcia said Detective Sergeant Gillespie told her he was in ICU and unconscious. Sorry Jennifer, we didn't want anything to spoil your trip."

"I appreciate you all felt that way. It comes as no surprise with poor Jorge—actions have consequences. He made some bad choices." She paused. "Still, though, one hates to see anyone go through that kind of trauma."

She decided to change the subject. Tomorrow morning she'd make that phone call. But for now, she wanted to hear what was happening at work.

"Marcia met with Chaplain Clive Griffith right after you left. He stopped by the funeral home to discuss a family he had been working with. Tourists from the States. He was an older gentleman who had wanted to see the Falls all his life. His parents were married in Niagara Falls; he was told many times by his mom that he was conceived there on their honeymoon. His daughter and her husband brought him to the Falls and they did the Maid of the Mist and Table Rock. He was thrilled. The family checked into their hotel after a busy day and he suffered a stroke. He died a few hours later."

"Oh," Jennifer responded. "That's sad, and sweet at the same time."

"Marcia will fill you in. She sat down and cried after the family left. The coroner's call was a car accident." His tone changed. "It's the first time I have been to a scene like that. It was awful."

Jennifer sat in silence for a minute. She knew Marcia would be sensitive to Peter's shock and horror. What she had never told him was that one doesn't ever get used to it. If they appear to, then chances are they have shut down emotionally.

"I'm sorry Peter. It doesn't get easier."

"No?"

"No."

He took a deep breath and exhaled slowly. "Even though it was just the police at the scene when we got there, it felt like it just happened. He was my age. His stuff, loose change, his shoe, a coffee cup that said something like 'I can't adult today.' The mug didn't break but he died." Peter paused. "Kinda shook me up."

Jennifer didn't respond. Peter had his wife and son and a baby on the way. The coroner's call had hit him hard; one second was all it took to end a life.

A minute later Peter continued.

"The cremation was direct, no service. The family picked up the remains yesterday. The other two services took place on the same day. That was fun."

"How so?" asked Jennifer.

"Details. Dozens and dozens of details. Marcia had Drew come in and help her in the prep room. He drove limo for the church service and even with the four of us we could have used an extra pair of hands. Elaine didn't miss a beat. It was flawless. Marcia was saying that when you guys worked in Toronto you could be doing six or seven funerals a day."

Jennifer chuckled. "Not the two of us, per se, but yes, once in a while you would have a dry spell then a run of calls. The most I remember doing was ten calls in one day. Course, we had the staff and sister funeral homes from the corporation sent over support staff. We would get sent out from time to time if the sister funeral homes were busy. I didn't like the high volume; it didn't give us much of a chance to get to know the families."

"Remember I said there's something I wanted to tell you?" said Peter.

Jennifer looked over at him. It was dark, they were on the highway but even in the darkness she could tell he was serious.

"Angel and I have talked a lot about this," said Peter. "I have applied to Humber to become a funeral director."

Jennifer wasn't quite expecting that. She thought Peter was going to say he was quitting. She realized she had been holding her breath since he'd said there was something he wanted to tell her. She exhaled.

"I'm not surprised. I saw your face when we picked up the pit boss. Uncle Bill believed that funeral directors are born, not just made. You were born to serve families."

"Thank you," said Peter humbly. "It's like I have to do it. I have watched you closely and am really moved at how you help people. You give up so much of your own time for them. And it seems like the more you give the more content you are."

"Sometimes," said Jennifer with a smile. "There are times when I resent the intrusion, I get tired, we all do. It can be hard to find a balance. It helps to surround yourself with like-minded people. One of the things I noticed when working in Toronto, it seems like there are two types of funeral directors: those who go to work every day and collect a paycheck, and those who make it a life calling. Course, that's just my opinion."

"I think you might be right. Take Drew for example. Even at work he's talking about what he's planning on doing on his day off, how he's going to get the latest video add-on for his games, his new girlfriend. Not that one shouldn't enjoy life. He just seems almost, almost …" Peter paused, searching for the right word. "Oblivious. There are people grieving around him and he's chattering about other things. He doesn't seem to notice them."

"Maybe that's his way of coping. I suspect he won't stick it out long. Perhaps his family was in the business and wanted him to be a funeral director, or maybe he just picked it because it seemed like a cool thing to do."

"He's into zombies and fantasy and war games," said Peter. "I got an earful at the last service when we were waiting outside the church."

"He's young."

"Marcia thinks he's lazy and disorganized," laughed Peter. "I think Marcia is the Iron Lady of funeral service. She's all business and attention to detail and about putting the family first. She took him aside twice during that funeral to straighten him out. I don't think he was impressed."

"Marcia and Phil were my mentors, as was Uncle Bill. I'll never stop learning. They gave me a good strong foundation and I look up to them." She sighed. "Looked. Uncle Bill was very different from Marcia, and Phil is different from both of them as well. I miss Uncle Bill. You will find your own voice and style Peter. I know you'll be a great funeral director."

"Thank you. I'll do my best."

"Not to jump too far ahead," Jennifer said lightly. "But when you finish your first year, you have a home-grown apprenticeship with us, if you want it. Another option might be a big city funeral home for an apprenticeship, you have the potential to become a manager in time."

"So did you," said Peter. "Would you have considered it if you hadn't inherited the funeral home?"

"No. Marcia and I talked about this many times. We enjoyed working directly with the families and apprentices and junior staff, well, mind you, I was junior staff. Neither of us had any interest in corporate culture or administration. I think Phil will be moving up soon. He blends beautifully into both worlds. It's good money, but it is a cutthroat business. There's lots of training and support, but nope."

"That reminds me, the manager from Williams Funeral Home was looking for you. Dimitri?"

"Dimitri, correct. Huh, wonder what he wanted."

"Elaine chatted with him for a few minutes, she'll know."

They pulled into the funeral home lot a few minutes before 9 p.m. Marcia met them at the garage entrance and the two of them hugged.

"Thank you for covering. Peter called you an Iron Lady," said Jennifer. Peter pretended to look guilty.

"I meant it in the nicest way possible."

Marcia laughed. "Time flew by. Let's get upstairs and catch up."

They said goodnight to Peter and started up the stairs. Jennifer could hear Grimsby meowing. She covered the last few steps quickly and opened the door.

"Oh, I missed you so much Grimsby," she said, picking him up and hugging him. Grimsby wasn't impressed. He wanted down. Jennifer laughed and put him down. Dumping her suitcase on her bed she came back into the living room. Marcia had started tea.

The two of them looked at each other.

"Well?" said Jennifer.

"It's been interesting. It's a lot harder when you're responsible for everything. I rather enjoyed the challenge though."

"Peter told me about your call with Chaplain Griffiths," said Jennifer.

"Oh my gosh," said Marcia. "He is the sweetest man. He's adorable. And the family, it's quite the story. Mr. Jones, and yes, his name is Jones, grew up in the south during the Second World War. He was an only child and his mother adored him. His dad worked as a farm hand and they were poor. He started working in the fields when he was ten. He had to quit school when he was twelve because his father was murdered."

"How awful," said Jennifer.

"It was a volatile time in the south, the Klu Klux

Klan was active. Mr. Jones' daughter said that her dad told her he used to hide in the fields when violence would erupt. His mother was a God-fearing woman who wouldn't let him grow up bitter and angry even though their house, which was barely a shack, was burned down more than once. She died when he was still in his teens. Mr. Jones served in Vietnam as a medic. He did several terms and was awarded more than one medal. On his last day, he lost his arm in an explosion while trying to save another soldier."

Jennifer sat silently, caught up in the life story.

"Eventually he met and married a young woman who had grown up in Atlanta. She was black too but her dad was a lawyer and involved in the civil rights movement. They had grown up worlds apart yet they were true soul mates, his daughter said. The daughter says she never heard a cross word between them. Her mom went on to distinguish herself as a lawyer and activist. Her dad, with barely a grade three education was intelligent and kind and generous to all. The daughter said her life was filled with music and books and joy growing up."

Marcia poured herself some more tea.

"Her mom was murdered one night leaving the courthouse after working late on a case involving the Klan and a rape victim. She was ambushed. They never caught the killer. When his wife died, her dad changed. He never seemed to stop grieving. He couldn't find work. They eventually ended up on the streets. He was a veteran forgotten by the system."

Marcia started to tear up. "Even at his lowest he cared about others, his daughter said. He had nothing but he gave everything. Her dad made sure she finished her education. She met her husband at college, they married and started their family. Her dad moved in with them and continued to help anyone who needed it. He volunteered at homeless shelters, churches, food banks. He'd pick up junk and sell it to get by."

"It almost doesn't sound real," said Jennifer.

Marcia nodded. "He used to tell his daughter over and over about his mother and father and their honeymoon in Niagara Falls. He said that during tough times when he was little his mother would talk about it with joy. His dream was to see the Falls and his daughter was able to eventually bring him here.

"As broken and shocked at his death as his daughter was, she was so happy to see the joy on her father's face his last day." Marcia paused. "They were such an amazing family. The daughter was surprised by the support they got from the people in their town. We know how costly repatriation is. The daughter said that money started flowing in the moment word got out that he had died. The town arranged for a veteran's funeral. The family paid the bill in full just before they left, from the donations. Peter and I took him across the border to the airport to be flown home.

"Chaplain Clive was there for them every minute he could be. The family adored him. He did a very tender and kind thing. He asked the family if he could hold a small memorial service at the Falls and he invited me and one of the nurses who looked after Mr. Jones to join them. Chaplain Clive took a small cross, talked about the impact Mr. Jones had in this world in a way that gave us goose bumps, prayed, then handed the cross to the daughter. She held it close, kissed it then dropped it over the falls as a memorial to her dad. The nurse and I were sobbing."

"In a perfect world he would have had the life he deserved, he would not have grown up surrounded by violence and hatred. He would not have lost his wife to such ugliness. His footprint in this world far exceeds yours or mine," said Marcia. "Every now and then a family changes your outlook on life. Mr. Jones did that for me."

"How could he not," said Jennifer thoughtfully. The two of them sat in silence for a few minutes.

"And the coroner's call?"

"Hmmm," said Marcia. "It happened shortly after you left. Peter handled it well and we debriefed after. He said he had done the homicide with you but it didn't affect him like this one."

"Did he tell you he has applied to go into Funeral Service Education?"

"Really? No surprise there. He has the heart for it."

"How's the condo search going, did you have time to look?"

"Yes, in fact, I've seen a few. I have a good lead on one tomorrow. It's in Ryan's building."

"Ryan? Is that your realtor?"

"No," laughed Marcia. "You've certainly seen enough of him over the past weeks."

Jennifer clued in, "You mean Detective Sergeant Gillespie."

"One and the same," responded Marcia. "I thought you'd have been on a first name basis by now."

Jennifer couldn't help but notice how her friend's face lit up as she talked about the police sergeant.

"I honestly didn't know his first name," said Jennifer. "So what's up with you two?"

"We're having dinner tomorrow night after we look at the condo. There's one in his building that's going on the market and if it's anything like his, I'll be putting in an offer they can't refuse. Perfect location, near the highway, I can be here in less than thirty minutes; it's close to the action but far enough away to be quiet."

"Like his? You mean you've been to his place?"

"He was just showing me the layout," said Marcia almost defensively. "He's such a neat freak, his place is spotless."

Jennifer was floored. The Detective Sergeant with the crooked grin and her friend. She didn't see that coming.

"How many square feet? Any amenities?" she asked.

"1300 sq. feet, indoor pool and fitness room, parking. t's on the top floor corner, a two bedroom with a sort of view of the mist from the falls. Nice grounds. The lady that's selling it has been there since the place was built. Ryan has kind of looked out for her over the years and she's happy to let me have the first look. The condo market is tight."

"I hope it works out for you." Jennifer meant both the condo and Detective Sergeant Gillespie. Marcia deserved every happiness.

Grimsby took that moment to jump onto the couch and settle beside his mistress. "Don't get too comfortable bud," said Jennifer fondly as she scratched behind his ears. "It's bedtime."

"We didn't even talk about your trip," said Marcia.

"Not much to talk about," laughed Jennifer. "It's Vegas. It was fabulous."

"Tomorrow I'll move into the cottage if that's

OK."

"Tomorrow is a day off for you. And so is the rest of the week and whatever else you need. I can call you if we get busy."

"I'll probably hang out at the funeral home when I'm not house hunting. I like it here," said Marcia.

Jennifer yawned and struggled to get up off the couch. "It's not late but it feels late," she said. "Bedtime for Bonzo."

"Oh, almost forgot, although Elaine won't forget. Dimitri was here to see you."

"Peter mentioned that. I'm curious, I'll call him first thing in the morning."

Jennifer soaked in the tub before heading into her room. Grimsby, ever fickle, had deserted Marcia and was curled up at the foot of her bed. Jennifer smiled at him, planted a kiss on his forehead and climbed into bed.

Ryan. He doesn't look like he should be named Ryan, he looks like a Douglas or a Matthew, she thought as she rolled over, pulled the covers over her eyes and drifted off.

13

Jennifer woke refreshed and alert early the next morning. She made coffee, had breakfast, and headed downstairs. Elaine had put all the files and messages neatly on her desk. She put the souvenirs for the staff at the corner of her desk to give to them later.

Logging in, Jennifer sipped her coffee and read the news. She played three hands of backgammon on one of her game sites, read her email, then looked at the messages on her desk. She reviewed the files, checked them against the computer and realized she was completely dispensable; the funeral home had continued on quite nicely without her. Just as it should, she thought. I can be replaced.

Promptly at 9 a.m. she picked up the phone and called Detective Sergeant Gillespie. To her surprise, she was put right through.

"Good morning," said Jennifer.

"Good morning Jennifer. How was your vacation?"

"It was perfect." She immediately launched into

the reason for her call. "I'm not sure if I'm out of line bringing this up, but I had an epiphany on the plane on the way home."

"How so?" he asked. She could feel the smile in his voice at her use of the word epiphany. For some reason, this time it didn't bother her.

"Did you or did you not tell me the night of the break-in that Jorge said the pit boss had given him the casket number?" she asked.

"I did."

"And I recall Jorge telling me he got that information from Travis," said Jennifer. "Speaking of Jorge, how is he?"

"Not responding. He probably won't make it."

"Did the pit boss have a name?"

"Roger Mitchell," he said. "So are you telling me you think Travis is involved?"

"I'm convinced Travis is involved. Travis stated he saw Mr. Mitchell put the money in the casket and he reported it to the police. Maybe Travis did see the pit boss, I mean, Mr. Mitchell, but not when he said he did. I wouldn't be surprised if it was Travis who put it there."

"Go on," said the Detective Sergeant.

"Jorge also said he and Travis *had a good thing going.* Travis travels the province taking over funeral homes for single owners so they can have a vacations or surgery or for whatever reason. It's the perfect cover.

I think Travis recruited Jorge. I also think Travis was the second in command. I also think Travis set Jorge up.

"That's a lot of 'thinks'," said Detective Sergeant Gillespie. "Any proof?"

"No," said Jennifer politely. "That's your job."

That was too much for Detective Sergeant Ryan Gillespie. He burst out laughing and didn't stop for a full minute. Jennifer heard Marcia coming down the hall.

"Is your sidekick up yet?" he asked when he recovered. He clearly didn't want to discuss Travis further.

"Marcia just came in. Would you like to speak to her?"

"Yes please."

Jennifer covered the receiver, "It's Detective Sergeant Gillespie for you," she said to Marcia as she handed her the phone and left the room.

"Hi Ryan," she heard Marcia say as she walked away. It was Jennifer's turn to smile. At least she'd given him something to think about.

Jennifer headed to the front office to say hi to Elaine and call Dimitri. Elaine was working at the desk, deep in thought.

"Hi Elaine." Elaine jumped to her feet and gave Jennifer a big hug.

"How was Vegas?"

"Incredible. Anne and I loved it. I'm ready to get back to work and put Jorge and Travis behind me. I have to call Dimitri; did he tell you why he was here?"

"No. He had me a little worried. Dimitri has aged over the past year and doesn't look so good."

"I thought he was looking unwell too," said Jennifer. "I'll call him now. Maybe there is something we can do to help."

She dialed Williams Funeral Home. A young woman answered.

"Jennifer Spencer calling. May I speak to Dimitri please?"

"He's not here." It sounded like the receptionist was chewing gum. Jennifer waited and listened. She was chewing gum. Jennifer was horrified. The receptionist didn't say another word.

"When do you expect him?"

"Dunno. Do you want to speak to the funeral director?" Finally, thought Jennifer, some initiative.

She was on hold for a bit longer than she thought necessary before Drew answered. At least he was professional.

"Drew speaking, how can I help you?"

"Hi Drew, it's Jennifer. How are things?"

"Not bad. How was your trip?

"Fabulous thanks. Is Dimitri in?"

"Not yet, he's usually in before me. Then again, haven't seen much of him lately. I can have him call you when he gets in."

"Thanks Drew. Talk to you later."

"Bye Jennifer." Drew hung up. Jennifer found Marcia and Elaine in the lounge.

"I can't believe the conversation I just had," said Jennifer. "The young woman who answered the phone at Williams Funeral Home had zero telephone presence and she was chewing gum."

Marcia laughed. "That's Stephanie. She's Drew's girlfriend. I don't know what Dimitri was thinking when he hired her. His previous receptionist quit last week to have a baby."

"Poor Dimitri. He's been the number one funeral home in town forever. If he keeps this up he'll start losing business. He and Uncle Bill were friends and there was mutual respect. Mind you, I'm being catty. It's none of my business if Stephanie doesn't meet my standards."

Jennifer felt a bit guilty. She knew she was prone to judge people quickly and wasn't proud of that part of her nature. She had a tendency at times to be an absolute thinker.

The front door chimed and Elaine went to check. It was a family who had walked in to make arrangements. Jennifer spent the rest of the morning working with them, transferring and getting ready for an evening visitation. Marcia helped for a while then packed up and left for the cottage. Jennifer put Dimitri out of her mind.

It was later that evening, as the family was leaving, that Jennifer remembered she hadn't heard from Dimitri. He probably didn't get the message, she thought. I'll try again tomorrow. She watched the last car pull out of the lot. She was locking the front door when a car pulled into the portico. A woman exited the car and came to the door. Jennifer opened it for her.

"Jennifer?" the lady asked. She looked like she was in her sixties, attractive and well dressed. She had a heavy accent and put Jennifer's name into three syllables.

"Yes, I'm Jennifer. Please come in."

"I'm Althea, Dimitri's wife." On closer inspection, as Althea walked in Jennifer thought the woman looked like she'd been crying.

She led Althea to the lounge, flicked on the lights and offered her tea or coffee. Althea chose tea and Jennifer made a cup for both of them.

"Thank you my dear," said Althea. "We must talk now." She started to cry.

Jennifer was slightly taken aback by the tears. She walked over to the counter and picked up a box of tissues.

"Dimitri sent me. He needs to know tonight. He

had a heart blockage last night, the doctors must operate."

"Oh no! I'm so sorry."

Jennifer's text chimed. Jennifer glanced at her phone; It was Marcia telling her she was on her way over.

Come 2 lounge ASAP, Jennifer texted back and turned off her phone, apologizing to the crying woman.

"Dimitri wanted to see you. He must take a rest. We were to go to Greece for a few months. He needs to go. Now he has an operation." She continued to cry.

Jennifer sat quietly with Althea. Five minutes passed. She heard the front door open and Marcia joined them.

"Althea, this is Marcia. Marcia, Althea is Dimitri's wife. Dimitri has a heart blockage and has to have surgery."

"You ladies, you help?" said Althea, her accent heavy. "Dimitri can't work; he must get better so we can go to Greece."

Jennifer didn't quite know how to respond. Althea mistook the silence as a negative.

"We pay, we pay well, please," said Althea.

"This isn't about money Althea, it's about what you need. Can you give Marcia and I a couple of minutes to talk?" asked Jennifer.

"You talk, I wait. Dimitri must know tonight. My Dimitri, he could die."

Marcia and Jennifer walked out to the hallway. Neither of them spoke for a few seconds. Marcia broke the silence.

"That poor woman," she said. Jennifer nodded.

"I think we need to look seriously into whether or not we can make a long-term commitment at this point," said Jennifer. "If Dimitri does well after surgery he should be able to talk to us in about a week. What do you think Marcia?"

"I agree. Can we do this?"

"It's so unexpected. Would you be comfortable working there with Stephanie and Drew?"

Marcia raised an eyebrow. "Didn't Peter call me the Iron Lady?"

In unison, the two of them said quietly, "We got this."

They walked into the lounge together.

"Althea, of course we will help. Marcia will go over and work with Drew and Stephanie for a week. When Dimitri is able to talk again we will discuss the situation a week or so from now. Are you OK with that?"

"You good girls, thank you," sobbed Althea. "I tell Dimitri now before operation." She rose and hugged Jennifer, then Marcia.

Walking out Althea did her best to compose

herself. She turned to them. "A corporation came to buy our business. Dimitri did not want them to buy. Too much stress, too busy, then Jorge …" Her voice trailed off.

"You such good girls."

"Althea, don't worry. There's no rush to make any decisions. What hospital is Dimitri in?" asked Marcia.

"St. Catharines. They moved him there tonight for operation."

"Then you go to him. Do you have keys for the funeral home?" asked Marcia.

"Keys. I forget keys. You come to the funeral home, I give you keys."

"We'll follow you over if that's OK with you," said Jennifer. Althea nodded.

All three women left the building. Althea got into her car. Jennifer and Marcia locked up and drove over in Marcia's car. When they arrived at Williams Funeral Home Althea was bustling about, tsk-tsking and fussing.

"This mess, this is not my Dimitri. Look at this. Look." She ran her finger along a table. It was dusty. "The shame."

She turned to Marcia. "You fix. my Dimitri don't do this." Marcia smiled, as Althea's frustration grew, her cultural mannerisms became stronger.

"I'll make sure that when Dimitri is strong

enough to come back to work, his funeral home is the way it should be. I promise."

Althea entered the front office and erupted into a string of Greek. Jennifer and Marcia were taken aback. The garbage was overflowing, there were candy and gum wrappers on the desk and magazines were strewn about. Donation cards were haphazardly jammed into the rack. A drawing of something resembling a zombie was lying in the open. It was sinister and hideous.

"Ack!" yelled Althea snatching up the picture. It hadn't been that bad the last time Jennifer was in. Clearly with Dimitri unable to keep an eye on things, Stephanie had made the office her own and it wasn't good.

"Whoa," said Marcia exhaling.

"Oh dear," said Jennifer.

Althea snatched up the zombie drawing, crumpled it into a ball and jammed it into the garbage. She turned to Marcia and Jennifer.

"This will stop now." She stamped her foot. "You make it stop."

Marcia, who was at least six inches taller than Althea straightened up. "It stops now Althea. You have my word."

Althea opened the desk, pulled out the keys and dropped them into Marcia's hand. "You girls do what you have to do. I go to Dimitri now." She turned and walked out the door.

Marcia retrieved the zombie drawing from the garbage. "Stephanie and I will be having a little chat in the morning," she said. "We probably should both be here. Hard to believe she took over after a week on the job."

Jennifer nodded. "I'm going to do a quick walk through and take some pictures just in case. We have no legal contract. I suspect Stephanie and maybe Drew will make a fuss; Dimitri has part time-staff who may not like the situation either. Have you meet his fleet manager?"

Jennifer shook her head. "No, I don't even know how many funeral vehicles he has to lease out. I'll look into it."

"I'm interested in one thing only," said Marcia. She looked at Jennifer. "This place will look and run like a funeral home when Dimitri walks back through that door."

Jennifer and Marcia did their walk through. Dimitri's office was a mess, contracts and paperwork strewn all over. There was an overflowing ashtray.

The suites weren't too bad, dusty but not messy. The lounge hadn't seen a good cleaning for a while, coffee cups were piled in the sink, garbage was overflowing, the floor dirty.

The prep room caught Jennifer off guard. It had not been cleaned since her visit with Drew. She was horrified. Funeral homes were inspected regularly. An inspector would shut down the funeral home the second he saw that prep room, let alone the rest of the facilities.

She and Marcia made sure she had good pictures of each area before they locked up and went back to Spencer's. Only then did she and Marcia sit down and talk.

"I think I'll bunk here for the night."

"You might want to leave some underwear and a few clothes in the dresser," said Jennifer. "You and I could have some long days and nights ahead of us. I can't believe what just happened."

"Me either," said Marcia. "Let's just make one thing clear. Althea did say something about making it stop, correct."

"She did," responded Jennifer. "Do you think you can teach Stephanie what a work ethic is and how to be a receptionist?"

"I can, but I think there's someone else who can do it better." She smiled. "It's an Elaine job."

"And Drew?" asked Jennifer. "He's teetering on the edge of losing his license with that kind of behaviour."

"He's mine," said Marcia resolutely.

"Dimitri will probably not be back to work for weeks, maybe months. I'll call Mr. Duncan in the morning and discuss the situation with him. I want it in writing."

"You be the legal beagle," said Marcia. "As long as you are there when we meet with Drew and Stephanie tomorrow, I'll gladly take care of the rest. By the end of the week you'll see Williams Funeral Home as it should be."

"Then let's get to bed. I think we need to get there well before Stephanie and Drew tomorrow. Oh yeah," said Jennifer, "how was the condo and your dinner?"

"The condo is perfect. I don't want to look further. It needs paint and curtains and could use some new carpet. I told Ryan over dinner I'd put in an offer. He's going to let the lady know. As for dinner …"

She paused and cocked her head to the side. "What did you say to him this morning? He was interrupted during dinner by a phone call, which he took outside."

"I told him I thought Travis was involved and gave him a few reasons why. Maybe it was another case distracting him."

"When he came back in he asked me when you moved into this apartment. Why would he ask that?"

Jennifer chewed her lower lip thoughtfully. In her best Vivian Leigh imitation, she responded with the classic, "I can't think about that right now, if I do I'll go crazy. I'll think about that tomorrow."

Marcia burst out laughing.

"Seriously Marcia, it's not my problem anymore. We have more important fish to fry."

Marcia continued to laugh. "You have the funniest expressions Jennifer. I think you meant to say 'bigger fish to fry.' Anyway, he mentioned something about your move and calling you."

"My bed is calling me. Grimsby, who do you want to sleep with tonight?" Grimsby looked at her and didn't move.

"Good night Marcia, good night Grimsby," she said as she headed for the bathroom.

"Good night Jen," said Marcia as she flicked on the TV, her way of winding down.

14

By 8:30 the next morning Marcia and Jennifer were at Williams Funeral Home. They had paid extra attention to their suits, hair, and makeup. They went into the lounge, replaced the expired creamers and milk, washed and put away the dishes, scrubbed the counter and dusted. They swept and mopped the floor and made coffee. At 9 a.m. they poured themselves a cup, sat down, and waited.

It was 9:15 before they heard the door open. Drew and Stephanie were giggling and thumping as they entered. It got really quiet really quickly.

"What's going on," they heard Drew say to Stephanie. "I didn't see Dimitri's car. Why are the lights on?"

"Hey," said Stephanie. "Someone's been messing with my office."

Jennifer and Marcia continued to sit quietly. They heard Drew moving through the funeral home. They were a little surprised when they heard music coming from the front office. Stephanie had added some additional flavour of her own, some hard core rock music.

It took almost ten minutes for Drew and Stephanie to find their way downstairs. Drew paled when he saw Marcia and Jennifer. Stephanie just glared.

"Who are you?" she demanded. "What are you doing here?"

Marcia and Jennifer rose. Stephanie looked them up and down in disgust. Stephanie was wearing black jeans with black combat boots, a black t-shirt and considerable body jewellery.

"Good morning," said Marcia pleasantly. "Please take a seat. We are going to have a staff meeting."

Jennifer would have laughed if the situation had not been so serious. Drew looked dreadful; she thought he was going to pass out.

"Before you pour yourself a coffee and join us Drew, would you be so kind as to go upstairs and turn off the music?" continued Marcia.

Drew actually tripped going up the stairs. The music ceased abruptly.

"Hey," said Stephanie. "You don't go messing with my stuff." She didn't appear to be one bit fazed by Jennifer and Marcia.

Jennifer sat down, Marcia remained standing. As Drew came back down she watched him scan the fresh, clean lounge. He walked over and sat beside

Stephanie.

"We're here at Dimitri's request," said Marcia. "Dimitri's in the hospital and asked that we help out. His wife specifically asked that we fix this situation."

"That cow?" said Stephanie. Jennifer could see Drew subtly elbow Stephanie, who glared at him.

"Drew," continued Marcia. "Jennifer and I have observed that there are considerable violations under the Act, several serious. I am sure you are aware that your license could be on the line."

Turning to the defiant young woman Marcia continued. "Stephanie," she said in her pleasant, even tone, "can you tell me what training you have? I wasn't able to locate your resume."

Stephanie, who matched Marcia in height, tried to stand up. Drew pulled her back down. Stephanie jerked her arm away and told him to stop.

"I finished high school," said Stephanie. "It's none of your business."

Marcia continued. "Are you willing to go home and put on appropriate business attire until we can order you a suit? If you go home and change, *and* if you are willing to take some training, I have someone who will work with you to help you improve your skills."

An angry and defiant Stephanie leapt to her feet and confronted Marcia. "I sure as hell am not going to wear a suit. I don't want to look like you, you ugly old witch. Dimitri's going to hear about this."

"You can tell him all about it when he returns," said Marcia calmly. "If you don't want to accept the offer of assistance and business attire, then I will have to ask you to leave. I will make sure your unemployment forms and final pay are mailed out this afternoon."

Stephanie whirled around to the almost cowering Drew. "Get them out of here," she demanded

"Stephanie," he pleaded. "Please stop."

"No, you stop! They can't make me."

"Stephanie, this is a funeral home. Anyone could walk through that door at any minute. Please lower your voice," said Marcia in the same calm, even tone.

Jennifer felt like she was watching a bad movie. She could hardly believe what was taking place. Marcia impressed her to no end. Stephanie scared her.

"Come on," said Stephanie to Drew. "Let's go."

To Jennifer's surprise, Drew got up. Marcia was ready.

"Drew, if you walk through that door I expect that means you won't be returning," she said. Drew hesitated.

"You can't fire Stephanie. If she goes, I go."

"Here are your options Drew," said Marcia. "You are a licensed funeral director who is responsible for more than one serious infraction under the Act. You are responsible for this funeral home and the families you serve. You dropped the ball. If you stay you will be on probation and under my direct supervision."

"When is Dimitri coming back?" asked Drew sullenly. Stephanie pulled at his sleeve.

"It could be a few months," replied Marcia.

"Then I quit."

"I will take your keys after you collect your things," said Marcia. "Your Record of Employment and pay cheque will also be in the mail this afternoon. I will be filing a complaint with the Board with supporting documentation. You will hear from them."

Stephanie wasn't quite finished, "And you will be hearing from my lawyer."

"Have him address your complaint to this address, to my attention," said Marcia as she pulled a Williams Funeral Home business card from her pocket. "My name on the back."

Stephanie snatched the card and dragged Drew up the stairs. Jennifer and Marcia followed. Marcia stayed with Stephanie as she threw her things into a bag; Jennifer went with Drew to collect his things. Drew didn't say a word. Jennifer didn't trust herself to speak. She was very disappointed in him.

At the door Marcia asked Drew for his keys. He handed them over.

"Stephanie, do you have keys?" she asked. Stephanie didn't respond.

It was Drew who spoke up, "Give her the keys, Stephanie."

Stephanie dropped her keys into Marcia's outstretched hand. The door slammed behind them and a minute later Jennifer heard the squeal of tires as Drew sped out of the lot in his new car. Only then did she take a deep breath in and out.

"Oh my word. You were magnificent, Marcia. I'm shaking."

"Me too. It's a good thing we planned out all possible scenarios. I really wasn't expecting Drew to quit. He has a new car and rent and girlfriend to support. Honestly, I think he's an abused boyfriend. Stephanie's calling all the shots."

"I guess I should let Elaine know what's going on and get back to the funeral home. Do you want me to send Peter over?" said Jennifer.

"Yes please. We have a lot to do in short amount of time. I'll call Elaine with the details so she can get the pay and employment records out today."

"I'll be back later, after I go to the crematorium," said Jennifer. "Elaine can reach me if we get a call. I'll start looking for a new funeral director, document what took place today and call Mr. Duncan."

"This is going to be fun. I'm a manager of a funeral home, at least for a while. I never thought that could happen."

"You helped teach me much of what I know," said Jennifer. "For the next while you're no only my employee, but my competition. I'm worried."

The two friends laughed together. "See you later Marcia," said Jennifer as she closed the door behind her.

Back at Spencer's, Elaine greeted her happily, "How's it going?"

"You won't believe what I'm going to tell you. I have to document all of it. A few calls to make first though."

"Detective Sergeant Gillespie just called. He'd like you to call back ASAP."

"OK. I'll call Peter, then him, then I'll go to the crematorium, then I'll sit down with you and tell you what happened. I recorded it on my phone so I wouldn't forget the details."

"Sounds intriguing."

"It's like a bad movie. More drama than I've seen in years."

Jennifer went to her office and called Peter. "Marcia will give you all the details," she said.

"Thanks for helping out."

"I'll text Marcia and let her know I'll be there in a half hour," said Peter. "See you later."

She then called the police station. Detective Sergeant Gillespie asked if she could be at a meeting at the police station at 3 p.m., the major crimes unit wanted to review a few items with her. Jennifer smiled to herself. "If I don't have a call between now and then, I'll be there," she said. "I'll let you know if I can't make it. Oh, by the way, you can reach Marcia at Williams Funeral Home for the next few weeks or months. She'll fill you in on the details. See you later Detective."

She called Marcia to let her know about the meeting at the police station and said she'd try to stop by after.

Jennifer and Elaine loaded the casket from the call from the night before into the van and Jennifer headed off to the crematorium, grateful for the alone time the drive gave her. She needed to clear her head and organize her thoughts.

"What a crazy twenty-four hours," she said aloud. It wasn't like this in Toronto. If this is what owning a funeral home is like I need a thicker skin and better running shoes, she thought.

The drive there and back calmed her down. Elaine had lunch ready when she got back to the funeral home. "I had Peter stop by and pick up some sandwiches for him and Marcia," she said. "Now what's going on?"

Jennifer settled into her favourite club chair in the lounge.

"Have you met Althea, Dimitri's wife?"

"I have. Althea is a wonderful lady," said Elaine. "She's the power behind the throne so to speak. Dimitri doesn't make a move without consulting with her. She's one astute business lady."

"I liked her too." Then Jennifer told Elaine about Althea's visit and Dimitri's illness.

"Oh no. Have you heard anything since last night?"

"No. Do you feel up to calling the hospital and seeing if Dimitri has a room or better yet, leaving a message for Althea?"

"I definitely will," said Elaine.

"Thank you. If you're talking to her, let her know she has nothing to worry about; Marcia has everything under control. Now for the rest of the story."

"There's more?" said Elaine. "Isn't that enough?"

Jennifer told Elaine about the situation they found at the funeral home last night and showed Elaine the pictures.

"Dimitri could lose his license for that," said Elaine. "How could it get so bad? I can hardly believe it. That's not Dimitri's style, he'd never let that happen. Your Uncle would turn in his grave if he knew his friend was going through this."

"I couldn't understand a word coming out of Althea's mouth last night when she saw it," said Jennifer. "It was Greek to me, pardon the pun. I can guarantee she wasn't amused."

"Dimitri must have been very ill for a while to let things get away from him," said Elaine sadly.

"Althea gave Marcia and I full permission to 'fix' things. I told her we would go on a short term basis, maybe a week, until she was in a better position to make a decision. Apparently a corporate funeral home is looking at acquiring Williams."

Elaine recoiled, "That will never happen while Dimitri is alive. Dimitri and Bill made a pact that they would never, ever, sell to a corporation. Not that corporations are all bad," said Elaine meekly. "You and Marcia worked corporate. It's just not what either of them wanted."

"I understand. Not every funeral home should be corporate. I agree with Uncle Bill and Dimitri on this one. There's a pride of ownership and community at stake. So," continued Jennifer. "Early this morning after strategizing, Marcia and I put our stripes on, fussed over our hair and makeup and went to the funeral home early. We had the lounge spotless by 9 a.m. Drew and Stephanie were late. I didn't have their permission to tape this, it was more for my record keeping, but this is what took place."

"I understand. You won't hear a peep out of me."

Jennifer clicked on her phone recorder and the two of them listened to the playback. Once or twice Elaine gasped. When the recording finished Elaine sat back in her chair, her jaw slack.

"I can't believe what I just heard," she said. "I just can't believe it."

"Marcia was magnificent, wasn't she? I couldn't have done it. She would make a great lawyer. And speaking of lawyers, I think I need to give Mr. Duncan a call."

"I think that's a wise move. If you do need to work for Dimitri for a while you might want to cover all your bases. I'll call the hospital."

The two of them headed to different offices. Mr. Duncan took her call and agreed that some kind of documentation should be in place. He reassured Jennifer as well that Stephanie's threat had no merit. Jennifer told him she would send the photos and documentation of the conversations with Althea, and Drew and Stephanie. He promised to get back to her in a few days with a letter of intent. Jennifer appreciated his usual calm demeanour and matter-of-fact approach.

She checked the time. It didn't take her long to

get the information ready for Mr. Duncan. Her transcript of the conversation was accurate and nearly verbatim. She uploaded the photos and sent all the information to his office. She then deleted the recording.

Elaine let her know she had not been able to reach Althea, and that Dimitri was in the Coronary Care Unit. She left a message for Althea to call.

"I'll make a note to get Althea's cell number if she calls," said Elaine.

"I just got everything off to Mr. Duncan," said Jennifer. "And I deleted the recording. Now I have to start looking for a new funeral director for Williams. I don't think Marcia and I can handle the two places alone. Do you think you could hire a receptionist?"

"I think that can be done," said Elaine. "I'll get right on it."

Jennifer drafted a letter of complaint to the Board about Drew. She and Marcia could go over it in detail later. She also wanted to check with Althea before she sent it. She called trade magazines and had them put an employment ad for a funeral director on their website.

Finally, with an hour to spare before her meeting with the police, she got up from her desk and made herself some tea. She needed to make sure her timeline was correct and she hadn't forgotten anything.

When she was done, she checked her hair and makeup, said goodbye to Elaine and drove over to the Division Office. She could have changed to her blue suit, but felt a bit more empowered in her funeral suit. She chose to carry a grey portfolio instead of a purse.

Promptly at 3 p.m. Detective Sergeant Gillespie entered the waiting room and asked Jennifer to follow him. He led the way to a small board room and closed the door. There were two other men in suits at the table.

"Gentlemen, this is Ms. Spencer. Jennifer, these men are with the major crimes unit of the OPP; they are wearing name tags with a first name only. They have a few questions for you." He pulled out a chair for Jennifer at the head of the table.

"Ms. Spencer, we understand you have some concerns about Travis Holden," said the one named Doug.

Jennifer looked straight at him. This time she knew she was right and she wasn't going to let anything or anyone intimidate her.

"I do." She opened the portfolio and passed around copies of a timeline and transcript she had drawn up.

"When did Mr. Mitchell, the pit boss, allegedly come to the funeral home to meet with Travis?" asked Jennifer.

Papers shuffled. "The day before you took over the funeral home," said the one named Dennis. Jennifer had a wild off the cuff thought fly through her head. Why did these guys pick fake names starting with *D*? Was it because they were detectives and it starts with *D*? Couldn't they be a bit more creative? She snapped back to the matter at hand.

"What time was the visit?" asked Jennifer.

"Around 2 p.m. according to Mr. Holden," said Dennis.

"I officially took over the funeral home on the first day of the month. However, I had complete access to the apartment six weeks before the official take over date. I was in and out helping Mr. Duncan settle the estate. That meant I had keys to the garage and apartment.

"Two days before the first, I arrived around 7 a.m. with a van full of boxes and started moving small items in. From the windows upstairs and from going up and down the stairs repeatedly, and in and out, I could see every side of the building. I could tell who was coming and going. I did *not* see a man in a suit enter the funeral home. There were no funerals over that two day period, no prearrangements.

The men remained quiet and unmoving.

"If Mr. Mitchell did come to the funeral home, it was after 7 p.m. I did see Jorge, at least I think it was

Jorge, drive up at one point on day one for a brief period. He didn't get out of the coach, Travis met him outside. He handed Jorge something, a paper or an envelope.

"Why do you think it was Jorge?" Doug asked."

"This is where I struggled," said Jennifer. "I think it was Jorge because it was the Williams Funeral Home coach. Can I prove it was Jorge? Other than the records at Williams Funeral Home that I was able to access this morning that show that Jorge was driving the coach that day, no. I wasn't looking that closely."

"Go on," said Doug. The men were listening intently and making notations.

"When I left around 7 p.m. Travis wasn't there. The funeral home was locked up and I wandered around checking it out."

"The next morning at 9 a.m. I was back with another van load of small stuff. Again I was up and down and in and out. I was there all day except for about half an hour, approximately 9:35 a.m. to 10:10 a.m. I went to Canadian Tire to pick up some hardware and paint and do a Tim's run. I did see a man and woman come in late morning. I can assure you it wasn't the pit boss."

"And you know that how?" asked Doug.

Detective Sergeant Gillespie stepped in. "Because she did the coroner's call and saw him."

The two crime unit officers looked at each other.

"The family didn't stay long, and they left carrying cremated remains."

"At any point did you have a conversation with Mr. Holden?" asked Doug.

"Several times"

"What did you discuss?"

"Anything and everything but funeral home business. That was on the agenda for the next day. It was basically small talk, weather, Grimsby …"

"As in the town?" asked Dennis.

"As in my cat," said Jennifer, with a little smile. Detective Sergeant Gillespie couldn't hide his grin.

"Your cat?" said Dennis.

"Grimsby was going to stay in the garage in his carrier while the movers took the big stuff in. I wanted to be sure Travis wasn't allergic to cats."

"Continue," said Doug.

"Again, when I left that evening around 7 p.m. Travis was not in the funeral home."

Dennis sneezed. Absently Jennifer responded with, "Bless you."

Doug continued. "What time did Travis leave the funeral home both evenings?"

"Both nights? Promptly at 5 p.m." She wanted to tell them to look at the timeline, it was all there and she wondered if they were trying to trip her up. She knew she was being truthful.

She continued. "The day I took over the funeral home, the first of the month, the movers and I arrived at 7 a.m. They had been hired to provide full service, so once I oriented them as to furniture placement, I came downstairs. Grimsby was in his carrier and at the back of the garage. Travis came in at 9 a.m. I was in my funeral suit and ready to work. He didn't look pleased, although he remained pleasant. The locksmith came an hour later. Travis walked out to the garage shortly after the locksmith left, he said he wanted to get some air. I followed him out to check on Grimsby. He saw the new latch. I didn't see if he reacted, but Grimsby did."

"What do you mean?"

"He hissed at Travis. Grimsby did not like Travis."

"Ms. Spencer, do you expect me to believe your story based on the reaction of a cat?" asked Doug, barely disguising the sarcasm in his voice.

"I don't expect you to believe anything I say," responded Jennifer pleasantly. "I am merely outlining the facts as I observed them."

She continued. "Mr. Duncan, the solicitor, came in at noon. At no time was Travis out of my sight except for a very brief period. He was in the little office off the lounge going over the files with me. My phone rang, I excused myself and went into the lounge. I had my back to the office. There were keys in the drawer. If Travis was to take a key that was his opportunity and I think he took advantage of it. There was one key missing, one for the garage door. I didn't notice it until days later. Travis couldn't get in the back door at night if I was home, it was latched from the inside. He had to wait until I was out of the funeral home when the latch would not have been in place. Now, why did Travis nearly run Detective Sergeant Gillespie and I off the road the night the Mr. Mitchell's body was found? He was leaving the Falls in a hurry. Who gave Jorge the home address for Mr. Mitchell?"

The men didn't answer.

"The timeline is as detailed as I could make it. I used the receipt from Canadian Tire to verify the time, the day before I moved in, the day Travis said Mr. Mitchell was at the funeral home. The rest of the information can be verified in the police reports. I put down everything I remembered from the first break-in and when Jorge came back. I don't know how many times I saw a Taurus across the road, it was more than five. In hindsight I should have attempted to get the license plate number. As I told Detective Sergeant Gillespie, Jorge told me he and Travis had a good thing going. He said that Travis had given him the casket number. Travis told your team Mr. Mitchell did." She paused. "I think Travis set Jorge up and I think Travis tried to kill Jorge on the pretext that he was going to pick him up after his escape."

Detective Sergeant Gillespie cut in. "Jorge died yesterday. That it was a hit and run is a given. Have you seen Travis' Taurus since?" he asked the major crime detectives.

"Why did Travis come down the hall towards the selection room the night Jorge broke in? He was supposed to assess the situation and unlock the garage door and let the police handle it. Was he trying to be a hero? I don't think so," said Jennifer. "I perceived him as a threat. He was a threat. He tried to grab me. I think Travis intended to kill me and then Jorge. The doors were locked. He would have had time. He could have said he tried to 'save' me and killed Jorge in the struggle. And why were he and Jorge yelling at each other as I ran to the front door?"

Jennifer looked at Detective Sergeant Gillespie. He returned her gaze, his eyes signalling his approval.

"Anything else gentlemen?" he asked.

"Not at this time," said Dennis. He and Doug rose. "Thank you Ms. Spencer, if we have any further questions we will be in touch." The two men left the room.

Jennifer sat back in her chair and looked at Detective Sergeant Gillespie. It was time to move on.

"Have you talked to Marcia yet?"

"She was busy, we talked briefly. We're having dinner tonight."

"It's been an interesting twenty-four hours," said Jennifer. "Marcia was spectacular. Now, if you will excuse me, I have to run."

Detective Sergeant Gillespie walked her out. At the door he said quietly, "I'll let you know what happens."

"Thank you." She was anxious to get back to Williams Funeral Home and check on Marcia and Peter. Once she got in the car she checked her phone. Elaine had texted her to say that Althea called; Dimitri's surgery went well and she had Althea's cell phone number. Jennifer entered Althea's number into her phone and sent it to Marcia.

Can't exactly send flowers to Dimitri, thought Jennifer. We see enough flowers in our work. Maybe I'll pick up a card on the way back and have all of us sign it.

She couldn't keep the smile off her face as she started the car.

"Gotcha Travis."

Winter's Mourning

The Spencer Funeral Home Niagara Cozy
Mystery Series
Book 2

Sneak Peek

1

Marcia and Jennifer didn't see it coming. The casket slipped from the hands of the two elderly pallbearers who were bringing up the rear and crash landed on the edge of the grave with a sickening thump.

The casket spray slid off, landing face down.

Peter did his best to stop the casket from smashing onto the lowering device, he was unsuccessful. The heavy unit landed on his foot.

The widow fainted, folding gracefully into the grass. Peter nearly passed out too, from pain. A strangled groan escaped his lips.

Both funeral directors were rooted to the spot, it was like watching a slow motion clip from a comedy scene, except it wasn't a comedy show. It wasn't funny. It was a funeral. *Their* funeral.

Jennifer was the first to react. She went straight to the widow, whose eyelids were fluttering like a goose's wings taking flight from the water.

Marcia was next, she headed straight to Peter, whose breath was coming in short gasps. "The pallbearers," he managed to say as he collapsed onto the wet grass.

Marcia turned to look at the pallbearers. One of

the men had his hand on his chest. He didn't look good. She got to the elderly man quickly, took him firmly by the shoulders and led him to the closest gravestone, easing him down gently.

"Do you have a heart condition?" she asked him.

He nodded.

"Nitro?"

He patted his pocket and Marcia wasted no time digging out the bottle of little pills and getting one under his tongue.

Fortunately, one of the family members snapped out of it and came over to help. "I'm a nurse," she said.

You're an angel, thought Marcia as she turned the poor man over to the nurse's expert care.

The widow had recovered enough to attempt to sit up. A couple of family members tried to yank her to her feet.

"No!" said Jennifer firmly. "Not yet." Jennifer was wondering if she should get the woman to lie down again so she could put her into the recovery position, but decided against it. The ground was muddy and the widow's suit was wet and dirty.

She looked around for the limo driver. He was staring at the scenario unfolding in front of him, frozen to the spot.

"Jeff," said Jennifer. "May I speak to you please?"

He didn't move. At least he looked at her when he heard his name.

"Now please," she said with more emphasis on the now than the please.

He sprang into action, slipping twice on the wet grass. "In the trunk of the lead car is an oxygen tank and mask. Here are my keys," instructed Jennifer quietly. "Don't run."

"Oh my, oh my," said another family member who was fluttering her gloves in the widow's face. Jennifer wanted to swat them and yell at her to stop it.

"It's OK ma'am. Mrs. Werther will be alright," Jennifer said instead.

She pulled her cellphone from her pocket and dialed 911. Peter was fully supine now, writhing in pain.

"Police, fire or ambulance …"

"Ambulance; the cemetery. Second street entrance, section 4, grave 13. We have a pallbearer with a heart condition and a funeral employee with a fracture. The widow fainted and we are administering oxygen."

For a few seconds the 911 operator didn't respond. She probably thinks it's a crank call, thought Jennifer as Jeff came up behind her and handed her the oxygen.

"Pull the wrapper off the mask. No, don't touch

the mask. Here, let me take it from the wrapper," she said. She put her phone down, placed the mask on the widow and slipped the elastic over the woman's head to hold it in place. The valve was tight, Jennifer struggled with it. Jeff reached over and helped turn it on. Jennifer heard the satisfied whoosh as the oxygen went to work. She picked up her phone. The dispatcher would have heard the conversation.

"Hello?" said Jennifer.

"The ambulances will be there shortly," said the dispatcher. "We dispatched two."

"Thank you," said Jennifer as she disconnected.

The minister moved up beside her. "I'll take over here, Jennifer, if you want to check on your employee. Jennifer rose and thanked him, then went over to Peter. Marcia was with the pale, unhappy Peter.

Jennifer stooped down. "Peter, I'm so sorry. The ambulance is on its way. I'll let Angel know." He groaned. Angel was Peter's wife. She was pregnant.

"What do you suggest we do now?" she said quietly into Marcia's ear.

"Run?"

Jennifer did her best not to smile. Marcia had a point.

"Let's see if we can proceed with the committal and let the cemetery staff take care of placing the casket on the grave. One of us will check for damages to the casket, which means we may have to make a trip back to the funeral home to replace it, with the deceased in it of course."

Marcia had a knack for being quite witty when confronted with difficult situations. Jennifer remembered her response the night the funeral home had been broken into. Marcia made her laugh then, and she was close to making her laugh now.

"I'll check with the minister right now," said Jennifer and she made her way back to the widow. The colour in Mrs. Werther's face was starting to return.

"Rev. Stone," said Jennifer. "There are two ambulances on the way. Perhaps we should proceed with the committal?"

"Excellent idea," he stated and he moved purposely to the foot of the grave. The casket was at the front of the grave with the flowers still upside down on the grass but he proceeded anyway. In his booming voice, he ran through the committal service in record time, the siren's in the background getting louder and louder. At the final amen, which could barely be heard above the shriek of the sirens, Jennifer saw the lights of the ambulances closing in. She took a deep breath to compose herself and calculated it would take about two minutes for the cemetery manager to show up.

Calmly she met the first ambulance crew. "The

gentleman lying in the grass has a fracture, the gentleman sitting on the gravestone has a heart condition, he's had one sublingual nitro and a nurse is with him. The widow is sitting on the ground with the oxygen mask on."

"Geez Louise, what the heck happened here?" one of the paramedics asked.

"A series of unfortunate events," said Jennifer, her shoulders slumping. Gone was the urge to laugh, now she wanted to cry.

It didn't take long for the ambulances to load up. Peter went first, followed by the pallbearer and the widow who shared the second ambulance. The mourner's started to head for their cars. Jeff took the remaining family members to the limo.

Marcia bent down, inspected the casket carefully and stood up. "It's broken," she announced to no one in particular.

She pulled back the fake grass covering the edge of the grave. "Ah ha," she said as she flipped it back further. "Do you see what I see?"

Jennifer could only nod.

The cemetery manager had been standing on the periphery waiting for everyone to leave. As the family entered the limo, he hurried across the grass.

"Ms. Spencer," he said in his annoying whinny voice. "What happened here?"

"Pallbearer mishap," said Jennifer.

"Well," said the officious little man. "Perhaps you should screen your pallbearer's better."

Jennifer looked at him. At that moment he was the most hated person in her life. "Perhaps, Mr. Whitney, your staff could do a better grave set-up."

"Precisely," said Marcia. "Look." She pulled back the fake grass used to hide grave hardware and pointed at the lowering device. "With the ground wet and soft after the recent rain, the cemetery staff had placed lumber under it, the boards helped prevent the sides of the grave from caving under the weight of the casket. The front of the grave had two boards, the back had none. When the pallbearers tried to place the casket on the lowering device it started a chain reaction. The casket crashed because the lowering device tilted forward from the weight of the casket. Peter had tried to get the men to lift the casket and move it back. It was too much for the elderly pallbearers. As they struggled to lift and move to the front of the grave one of the pallbearers tripped over the lumber and let go of the handle. A domino effect resulted, one by one they let go. It's been my experience," continued Jennifer in an icy tone that did not disguise her anger, "that four boards are used when the ground is soft." She didn't mention that it was her responsibility to check the grave set up ahead of time, she was hoping he would forget that part. Jennifer had missed the missing boards.

She heard a car pull up. Glancing over she saw a familiar face. Marcia saw it too. Mr. Whitney had his back to the road, he didn't see Detective Sergeant Ryan Gillespie get out and head quickly to the graveside.

"Well," said Mr. Whitney. "If you women would stop playing funeral director and stay at home where you belong, then the male directors who should have been here would have had the strength to stop the casket's fall."

"Marcia, Jennifer, are you alright?" asked the Detective Sergeant. "Dispatch called me."

Marcia wasn't alright, she was livid. "We are fine, thank you Ryan," she said sweetly. "Mr. Whitney was just suggesting that we women should stay home and stop playing funeral director."

Winter's Mourning

Available Winter 2016-17
Amazon * iBooks * B&N * Kobo

ABOUT THE AUTHOR

Jan Richardson was born in Toronto, Canada and has lived and worked in various parts of Ontario. Her original career choice was medical office assistant; her dream was to be a funeral director. Years passed, she fulfilled that dream and went to college, got her license and did a post graduate certification.

She left funeral service to adopt and raise her special needs granddaughter, having raised a special needs daughter it was a natural progression. Her first book was non-fiction, *The Making of a Funeral Director.*

Jan currently resides in the Niagara Region. "It's is a great place to live; one never gets tired of the falls."

Thank you for reading the Spencer Funeral Home Niagara Series. If you liked the book, please rate or review it—thank you!

You can find me on Twitter: @richardson.jan1 and Facebook: Janice J. Richardson

I would love to hear from you.

Made in the USA
Middletown, DE
30 July 2016